A HOUSE FOR ELIZA
The Real Story of the Cajuns

Constance Monies

Constance Monies

Cypress Cove Publishing

Visit www.AHouseForEliza.com for the author's blog, news and updates.

Published by:
Cypress Cove Publishing
PO Box 91626
Lafayette, Louisiana 70509
(337) 224-6576

ISBN-10: 1-936707-21-7
ISBN-13: 978-1-936707-21-8

Library of Congress Catalog Card Number: 2012950569

♦ Publisher and Executive Editor, Neal Bertrand
♦ Cover design and production by Elizabeth Bell, eBell Design, Lafayette, Louisiana
♦ Interior design by Jeremy Bertrand, Cypress Cove Publishing

On the front cover:

Eliza Landry Daigle and husband Gabriel Oscar Daigle at the time of their wedding. 1893, Lafayette, LA

To my mother
Mildred Daigle Monies

"Millie"

One of Eliza's children and
the wind beneath my wings

Introduction

Who are the Acadians?

Acadians are descendants of early French pioneers who came to North America in 1604, to establish colonies in and around Nova Scotia. Once these colonies were formed, this broad area was named Acadie. The early Acadians lived happily in Acadie for 100 years, until France lost the colonies to Britain in 1713 in the Treaty of Utrecht. Under British rule, the Acadians were forced to pledge their allegiance to Britain and renounce their religion, or face exile. They refused, and beginning in 1755, the Acadians were loaded onto ships and then dumped at ports along the Eastern Seaboard.

The exiles no longer had a country and were treated with contempt and hostility wherever they went. During this time, Louisiana was under the rule of a Spanish government that was friendly toward the French. This government extended an invitation to all Acadians to come to Louisiana. Miserable and longing to be with their families, approximately 3,000 refugees quickly made south Louisiana their home. Along the quiet riverbanks and across the vast prairies, the Acadians found a new life in the "New Acadie." They built towns, churches and schools, cattle ranches, and plantations. Now the Acadians were recognized as teachers, doctors, trappers, fishermen, merchants, farmers, plantation owners, and statesmen. Deep inside Louisiana they lived a life untouched by the outside world. To many, these people seemed

4

suspended in time. On the contrary though, a unique culture was born, and with it came the Cajun.

The years between the late 1800s and the time before World War I provided an incubation period for the Cajun culture. Many historians feel this was the last time the Cajun was free from outside influences. This isolation provided fuel for colorful stories about the Cajun way of life and eventually people recognized that all Cajuns were Acadians but not all Acadians were Cajuns.

The New Cajun

The events surrounding World War II rapidly changed the Cajuns and their culture. Parents no longer taught French to their children, and Acadians often hid the fact that they were Cajun. It was not cool to be a Cajun anymore. Newspapers and radio had stories of Cajuns portrayed as illiterate and poor, living in houseboats or shanties along bayous and rivers. This stereotyping continued into the early 80s, and was reversed when people realized the little towns founded by the Cajuns were cities now, and many Cajuns held responsible positions in government. In the 90s, enormous advances in technology around the world made the Cajuns famous. They had the best food, the most interesting culture, and more fun than anyone else on the planet.

Approximately 400,000 people of Acadian descent live in South Louisiana. The Cajun culture has survived for over 200 years, and the Cajuns themselves have been loved, immortalized, and misunderstood for an equal amount of time.

To know Cajuns you must first understand what it means to be a Cajun: There is nothing more important than faith in God, love from family and friends, and truth and justice for all people. Cajuns are happy with life. They respect their land and all their worldly possessions as gifts from God. They are undaunted by life's tribulations, great and small, and often find humor in the darkest of times. Once you truly understand the Cajuns, you will also understand why the Cajuns are still here.

Eliza Landry

Eliza Landry was born in 1876, to an upper middle class Acadian family living in the town of Côte Gelée, which is now Broussard, Louisiana. When she was seventeen, she met and married Oscar Daigle. He was the son of Louisiana Senator, Francois Daigle, and the owner of a large plantation on the out-skirts of Lafayette. Together, Eliza and Oscar raised 17 children during two world wars and the Great Depression. In spite of immense changes in their lives during this time, the Acadians continued to celebrate their unique heritage and customs. By the time Eliza died in 1958, the culture of the Cajuns was firmly established in Louisiana, and is today one of the most unique and memorable cultures in the world.

Acknowledgements

Special Thanks To:
Carl A. Brasseaux, author and mentor, whose expert knowledge of the history of the Acadians provided me with direction and confirmation of my efforts to write the true story of Eliza and Oscar Daigle.
Jim H. Bradshaw, journalist and friend, whose popular newspaper column, "C'est Vrai" gave me a unique and accurate view of over fifty years of life in Acadiana.

Thanks to these artists, authors and photographers who also inspired me:
Floyd Sonnier, *From Small Bits of Charcoal: The Life & Works of a Cajun Artist*
George Rodrigue, *The Cajuns of George Rodrigue*
Shane K. Bernard, *The Cajuns: Americanization of a People*
Orpha Valentine (1926-2011), *Lafayette: Its Past, People and Progress*
O.C. "Dan" Guilliot, *Images de Lafayette: A Pictorial History*
Mario Mamalakis, *If They Could Talk: Acadiana's Buildings and Their Biographies*
Barry Jean Ancelet, Jay Edwards, and Glen Pitre, *Cajun Country*

Thank you:

To all my cousins who sent me their memories of our childhood together and the grandparents we shared. You made *A House For Eliza* rich and special.

To my daughters, Cynthia and Catherine. You were my first critics, and in spite of the fact that the first manuscript had numerous mistakes, you said it was good.

To my husband, Phil, for all your patience with the long hours I spent writing, and rewriting. You never lost faith in me.

And finally, thanks to Neal Bertrand, author, publisher, and friend. You showed me what it means to be a published writer.

"San Francisco may have its steep hills, Chicago its windy Lake Michigan, and New York its skyscrapers, but Lafayette has its people. They are not just ordinary, everyday people but people called Cajuns, whose Acadian ways have woven steel-strong the cultural fabric of south Louisiana and Lafayette. Despite major outside influences, Lafayette has kept the best of its past while yet becoming a cosmopolitan area. Business transactions are still conducted over cups of strong Cajun coffee. From fur trading community to modern day city, Lafayette has kept her Cajun heart. May she never lose it."

Orpha Valentine (1926 – 2011) *Lafayette: Its Past, People & Progress*

CHAPTER ONE

"What was that?" Eliza whispered. She slipped out of bed and walked close to the open window. A full moon had risen and flooded the house with pale light. She heard voices and saw shadows moving across the porch and down the steps, and she could see several men carrying pieces of firewood to a buggy waiting under the old oak tree. Eliza reached for her husband's rifle and carefully opened the door. She stepped outside onto the porch, took aim at the men and fired three shots. The cries of the men echoed through the pastures. All that was left on the porch was the moonlight. Eliza looked at her husband, Oscar. He was still asleep and it was obvious the children were asleep also because there was not a sound from their rooms.

NO ONE EVER knew for sure whether Oscar Daigle meant to be riding in front of Eliza Landry's house on the exact day her father was painting the gate and chimney white, but that's exactly what it looked like. Before long, practically everyone knew Oscar and Eliza were going to be married.

"My gate looks good white, don't you think?" Charles Landry asked his neighbor.

"The message is obvious, my friend," the neighbor said. "How did you find out?"

"Pierre told me."

"Suppose it is not true, then you have painted your gate and your chimney for nothing."

"Well," Charles puffed, "Eliza cannot spend all of her life teaching catechism to other people's children. She has to marry sometime. If her brother is telling the truth, and Oscar Daigle has really told Eliza he intends to marry her, well then, I'm all for that."

"What do you know about him?"

"Not much yet, but you remember him, eh? He is the son of Francois and Leocade. Remember when Francois ran for senator? Remember we never thought he would win?"

"Yes, yes, my friend. But that doesn't make him a good match for Eliza," the neighbor replied, shaking his head.

When Charles looked down the street he could see Oscar riding with his brother in the surrey. Charles put away the buckets and paint brushes, and disappeared inside the house. From there he watched as Oscar stopped in front of the house and studied the chimney, then got down and touched the wet gate. He reached for his handkerchief to wipe the fresh paint off his fingers.

His brother laughed. "What does all this mean, Oscar?"

"Painting a gate and chimney white is just a custom, you idiot," Oscar replied. "It means one of Mr. Landry's daughters is eligible for marriage."

His brother looked at him and grinned. "Which daughter would that be?"

In the days which followed the trip to Côte Gelée, Oscar often thought about the time he first saw Eliza Landry. She was teaching catechism to the children at the Chapel of Saint John, walking among her students as they sat in the grass in front of the little church. He had gone to ask Father Richard to bless his baby girl. It was late afternoon, and the sunlight caught Eliza's hair, touching the long brown strands with gold. Her black eyes looked steadily at him, as though trying to understand what his presence with a baby meant that late October day.

Not long after, Oscar brought the baby with him once again to the chapel and Eliza's catechism class. Eliza had been told how sad Oscar was when his young wife died in childbirth, and how Oscar's mother had to help with the baby.

"Eliza, I want you to meet my little Regina," he said.

She looked at the baby. "She's so tiny," Eliza whispered. "How old is she?"

"She is already six months old, but she is a premature baby. She weighed only three pounds at birth."

Eliza studied Regina. The baby's eyes opened, and Eliza thought perhaps Regina was studying her also.

Before long Oscar was paying regular visits to Eliza. "Tell me, Oscar, what is your business?" Charles Landry asked, raising his brows as he waited for an answer.

"My mother, Leocade, was a Boudreau," Oscar said, "and she had a large piece of land which was part of a Spanish land grant. That land was divided between me and my four brothers. I manage my own part, which is quite large."

"What about your workers," Charles asked, "freed slaves, I suppose?"

"Yes," Oscar replied, "thirty men and women at harvest time. The best crop is cotton. But there is also sugar cane and corn."

Oscar looked around the parlor and gestured with his hand. "I make an adequate amount of money, but I have not yet built a house because a man without a wife does not need a fine house like this. But someday," he sighed, "I will have more than just a house on my land. I will have a smokehouse, a wine cellar, orchards with fruit of every kind, vineyards, and a pond filled with fat crawfish and sac-a-lait. I will have horses too, and cows and chickens, and a big barn."

11

"All this takes time, Mr. Daigle."

"Yes … and a reason to do it," replied Oscar.

Eliza appeared with a tray of fine china cups filled with black coffee. Setting the tray down in front of her mother, Eliza returned quickly to the kitchen.

Idea Landry handed Oscar a cup of coffee, and smiled politely. "I remember when the baby was born," she said. "Such a sad situation. How did you adjust, Mr. Daigle?"

"My mother has helped a great deal. Of course, I was not prepared for my wife's death. And my daughter was so tiny. We were all boys, and there was no one else but Mother who knew how to care for such a baby."

"And how is your baby now?"

"Healthy and content, and growing a little bit each day," Oscar replied, looking at his half empty cup and realizing his visit had almost come to an end.

"Mr. Daigle," Charles asked, "do you feel you are ready for another family?"

"I am ready, sir, to move on with my life," Oscar said.

Charles watched as Oscar walked out of the freshly painted gate and climbed into his fancy surrey. He snapped the reins and turned the chestnut colored horse to the east toward the bayou town named Lafayette.

Charles looked at his wife. "Idea, what do you think?"

She shook her head. "I don't know. I just don't know! I've been told that Leocade Daigle spoiled all those boys after Francois died. And you know very well how much I hate politics. Francois was a real politician to the very end. Which one of the boys inherited that, I wonder?"

12

"Don't you think Eliza and Oscar were brought up in the same way, my dear?" Charles asked. "Both children seem to have the same values."

"I suppose you are right," Idea replied, "but I hope he can give her the things she needs to make her happy. After all, we have provided well for her all this time."

"Do you mean that plantation life may not be for Eliza?" Charles asked.

"This is difficult for me to say," Idea replied, "but I do not think she will have the same life with Oscar that she has with us. She will be expected to run that plantation with Oscar. She will have only the workers to help her cook and clean and Lord knows what else. She will be expected to do exactly as Leocade did, ride horses and take care of the sick workers as though they were members of the family. Now you know that we always kept our children separate from those freed slaves. They are not like us and never will be." Idea's eyes were wet with tears and she looked away quickly.

"You may be right," Charles said, "but aren't you forgetting that Eliza is strong-willed and usually does the right thing? And," he added, "I am certain Oscar loves her."

"That is not a guarantee that Eliza will be happy," Idea answered.

~ ~ ~ ~

It was a crystal clear Sunday morning in February. When Charles Landry and his family arrived at the Chapel of St. John, he saw the familiar chestnut horse and the fringed surrey tied to the second hitching post in front of the little church. Eliza knew that

13

Oscar was inside, but she walked right past him. Oscar followed her with his eyes. She is as pretty going as coming, he thought.

The Landry family always sat in the first pew on the left, and was the first to receive communion from Father Richard. Charles watched as his children got in line, Marie the youngest with Mama Idea, Helen, Emelie, Edmond, Pierre, Eliza, and then the oldest, Alcide. The sounds of the communion and the smell of the wine and candles filled the chapel.

Eliza tried to remember what the gospel was about as she walked out of church. She knew her mother would ask to see if she had been paying attention. She had thought only of Oscar, and caught her breath when she saw him waiting on the steps of the church.

"Good afternoon," Oscar said to Idea and Charles Landry, as he took off his hat and winked at Eliza at the same time.

Eliza walked quickly to the buggy and helped Alcide lift the youngest children into the surrey for the ride home. "Mama, do you want to ride in the front or the back?" Eliza called out. Idea eyed the buggy which began to rock from side to side with the help of little hands and feet.

"I think I'll ride in the back," she answered. She sat in the middle of the children, and they suddenly grew quiet. Her effect was not always so instant, but with Charles holding the reins, there was a certain decorum which filled the air.

"Papa," Pierre chirped, "Alcide says he will ride standing up in the Courir de Mardi Gras."

"And what is wrong with that?" Charles asked. "Mardi Gras is a time for showing what you can or cannot do, as the case may be. Are you saying he cannot ride a horse standing up?"

14

Pierre hesitated then said, "He won't be able to catch the chicken if he stands up on a horse."

"Who says I won't jump down," Alcide shot back, "and chase that chicken around and around until I catch her by her tail feathers, and bring her to Mama for the gumbo?"

For some reason the horse decided to snort and snicker just about this time. Pierre burst into laughter and fell out of the buggy. He began rolling around on the ground and grabbing his sides.

Idea cried out, "Pierre, get up. You are in your best clothes. What are you thinking, rolling in the dirt like a pig?"

The journey to the house finished in silence. Charles remembered that he was a little boy when he first saw the Courir de Mardi Gras. The riders were dressed in colored silk shirts and pants, and they wore masks with the faces of women. When they rode into town, the horses sounded like thunder, and the dust rose in thick swirls from their hooves. They rode up to houses and demanded something for the gumbo pot. One of the houses threw out a chicken, which ran from the riders with such haste that she left a trail of white feathers.

Charles shut his eyes for a minute. He saw the crowds of riders, filling the streets and spilling into the yards in front of the houses. They were intimidating and loud, and seemed to be part of a circus suddenly come to town. Under those masks no one could tell if they were friends or strangers, and they could have been enemies. Then the Capitaine with his whip charged through the riders, standing tall on his black horse, his boots glistening as he balanced himself high above the crowds. He yelled to the riders to leave. The chicken had been caught, and now the Mardi Gras must begin.

An invitation to the dance

Monday morning came in like a cold breath of winter, filling the house with the smell of more rain. Eliza looked out the front window and wondered if today would bring her invitation to the dance. Helen told her that a boy riding a pony was delivering something to the houses on the street. Yesterday, Alcide told Eliza that his friend had been invited, and Eliza heard the dance was to be a fine one. It was eight days before Mardi Gras now, and this was usually the time for dances, especially for the young ladies and gentlemen who were not allowed to participate in the Courir. Eliza had hardly walked away from the window when there was a knock at the front door.

"Yes?" she asked, opening the door to find a small boy with a note in his hand.

"I have come to invite Miss Eliza to the dance," he said.

Eliza took the note from his hand just as Idea walked down the hall.

"I've been asked to the dance, Mama!" Eliza said.

Idea looked at the note, handwritten on fine white paper and tied with a purple and green ribbon across the top. It gave the date and time of the dance, "This Saturday, at half past six in the evening, at the home of Ma'mam Fontenot."

Having delivered the note and completed his rounds, the young boy disappeared on his pony just as rain began to fall, quickly erasing the hoof marks in the dust. Eliza walked to the girls' room and opened the armoire which she shared with her sisters.

She pulled out the skirt she made with her mother. It was dyed indigo blue, and Eliza always thought it was the prettiest skirt she

16

had ever seen. Eliza and her mother had worked together, late into the evening, each day for one week. The skirt was the first thing Eliza had ever made.

Also in the armoire was a white blouse and red corset which laced up the front. Idea had made those, and Eliza held them up to herself as she twirled in the bedroom. Tied to the ceiling were the shoes Charles had bought for her. They were made in France. Eliza slipped her moccasins off and tied the shoes on her feet.

By the end of the week, the rain finally gave way to sunshine, but the wind was still cold. Winter was stubborn this year and it threatened to make Mardi Gras day miserable. Many people in Côte Gelée were sick, and several had been taken to the hospital in Lafayette. There was talk of yellow fever and pneumonia, and old people and babies dying quickly, before anyone could help.

"What if one of us gets sick, Mama?" Eliza asked, touching her mother's shoulder as she sat at her sewing machine. "Will you go to Lafayette right away?"

Idea stopped sewing and looked at Eliza. "Don't worry. There are more cases of yellow fever and pneumonia in Lafayette than here in Côte Gelée. We will be all right."

"Do you pray that we will stay well?"

"Yes, every morning and every night," Idea whispered. "Go and iron your skirt for the dance, and stop thinking about all of this."

Eliza wanted to ask her mother if she thought Oscar would be at the dance, but instead she walked down the hall to the parlor where orange flames heated a flat iron sitting in the fireplace. She picked up the skirt and holding it to her waist, she danced to an imaginary waltz.

When Saturday arrived, the same young boy on his pony appeared again, carrying a long stick with a piece of purple and green silk tied to the end of it. He swung the stick as he rode, waving the little flag high above his head.

"Pierre!" Eliza called. "Come quickly. Follow him and see where he ties the flag."

Eliza's brother ran after the pony. The little rider turned the corner near the big oak with Pierre running behind him. The street turned once and then again, ending at the house of Ma'mam Fontenot. The boy stopped his pony and tied the stick with the flag to the big iron gate, and then disappeared around the back of the house. When Pierre rounded the last turn, the young rider was nowhere in sight, but he spied the flag tied to the gate. "Well," he whispered, gasping for breath. "What does that mean?"

Walking back home Pierre decided he would not tell Eliza what happened. When she met him at the door, he walked quickly into the house.

"Pierre! Where did he go?"

"I'm telling you, he just disappeared," he answered.

Eliza grabbed his arm and pulled him towards her. "What are you talking about? Just disappeared? You lost him didn't you! You're an idiot!" Eliza laughed. "You can't even follow a little boy on a pony. You'll never amount to anything!"

Pierre eyed her and then shook his head. "He disappeared, I'm telling you. All that was left was his purple and green flag tied to Ma'mam Fontenot's gate."

Eliza looked at her brother with fire in her eyes, and between clinched teeth she said, "That's all I need to know. The party will go on as planned, tonight at Ma'mam Fontenot's house. Apparently you are not invited."

Eliza left for the dance with her father and Pierre. Idea stayed home to take care of Emelie and Helen since both girls had suddenly developed a high fever. When Charles told Pierre he could only watch since he was not invited, Pierre said, "But Papa, I can dance as well as any man there!"

"You were not invited, and therefore, you cannot participate," Charles insisted. "If you do not want to watch, then stay home with Alcide and Edmond, and help your mother."

Eliza turned and looked at her father. "What is wrong with Emelie and Helen, Papa?"

Charles shook his head. "I don't know. They will be all right. It's just a cold." He whistled to the horse, and father, daughter, and son rode in silence. The sky was filled with stars, and somewhere in the distance, there was the faint sound of music.

Eliza had her pale pink moccasins on her feet, but in her lap she held her dancing shoes. She was wearing the blue skirt and white blouse with the red corset. Her dark hair fell in ringlets around her shoulders, spilling over the white blouse like pieces of brown silk ribbon.

It was seven o'clock when the buggy pulled up in front of the Fontenot house. As the threesome walked through the iron gate, Eliza looked up at the front gallery with its windows sparkling in the golden light from the lanterns. The air felt cool and clean, and a full moon was just beginning to rise over the rooftop. Eliza looked for the surrey with the fringe, but it was not there.

Sitting on the wide steps leading to the front door, she quickly removed her moccasins and slipped her good shoes on her stocking feet. Hiding the moccasins underneath the steps, she brushed her skirt with her hands, tossed her hair over her shoulders, and

walked into Ma'mam Fontenot's parlor. People were already dancing to the music of the fiddlers.

She was asked to dance several times before Oscar arrived. He
looked slim and tall in his brown capot, his wavy dark hair a
striking contrast to his blue eyes. He held his palmetto hat, shaking
hands with many of the men while his eyes searched the room for
Eliza. He found her just as the musicians began to play a waltz.

Charles walked into the dining room where Samuel Fontenot
and his friends were gathered around a makeshift bar. Imbedded
in the wall alongside the bar was a large knife with a hat hanging
on the handle.

"Mr. Fontenot," Charles said, "what do you say we ask the
owner of the knife and the hat to leave?"

Samuel Fontenot laughed. "You are right! He is a bully and
there will be trouble, unless, of course, he can't find anyone to fight
with."

"In that case," Charles replied, "he will probably fight with the
other bullies." The room broke into laughter then suddenly grew
quiet as Jean Breaux walked from the back of the room and
removed his knife and hat from the wall.

Now, this man was from a little town known for its rough
citizens called Marais Bouleur. Jean Breaux lived up to that reputa-
tion, and he and his brothers had been thrown out of some of the
finest parties in Lafayette.

"I am better than any man here," Jean shouted. "Whoever
disagrees, let him come forward so I can demonstrate."

Not one person in the room moved or said a word. Eliza
looked around at the men and women who were huddled in
groups. She felt as though her heart would stop at any minute, and
she would die right there in Ma'mam Fontenot's parlor.

"You, my friend, are drunk. Go home and sleep," Charles called out.

Jean Breaux laughed and doubled his fist, walking along the front row of men who now stood three deep across the wide dining room.

"Show me! Which one of you is better?" he snarled.

The crowd backed away, and Jean cried out again, "You let me win too easily! Come on, I am ready!"

"Take it outside." Charles said.

Jean planted his knife deep into the cypress dining room door which led to the outside, and ceremoniously hung his hat on the knife handle once again.

"You are right, Mr. Landry. I should go outside, and you should come with me so I can give you that little demonstration I promised." When Charles looked through the window he could see all of Jean's brothers waiting outside in the bright moonlight. Jean stepped through the door and motioned for Charles to follow. As soon as Jean was outside, Charles threw the knife and hat after him and quickly drew the bolts across the door.

"Look at him. He is a coward like all the others." Jean screamed out.

The dining room crowd returned quickly to the parlor and the music began again. Eliza realized she had not seen Pierre in a while. "Papa, where is Pierre?" she asked.

"Probably with the other children," Charles answered as he pointed to the hallway. "I have finished my gumbo," he hissed, "go and tell him it is time to go home."

~ ~ ~ ~

When Charles brought his son and daughter home close to midnight, the light was still burning in the girls' bedroom. Eliza ran past her mother to the door of the room and looked at her two sisters lying in their beds. Helen seemed to be sleeping peacefully, but Emelie was restless. Her face was pink and her breath came in gasps. "Mama, I am afraid," cried Eliza. "Have you been praying as you said you would?"

"Yes, I have," Idea whispered. "Alcide has gone for Doctor Gilbert. We must wait and hope. That is all we can do now."

"No, Mama, no! We must pray more. We cannot stop like this. We must pray more!" Eliza was sobbing now, on her knees with her hands tightly clinched.

"Idea, take Eliza to the parlor," Doctor Gilbert said as he walked into the room. "Let me have a look at these children."

Eliza slept fitfully in the parlor. Night turned into morning and she awoke with a start, remembering her pink moccasins left under the steps of Ma'mam Fontenot's house. She looked at the clock on the mantle. The glass door was ajar, and the pendulum was still. Someone had stopped the hands at four o'clock, and Eliza knew Emelie was dead.

CHAPTER TWO

DURING THE MONTHS which followed the funeral, Eliza thought many times about the little coffin draped in white. "Do God's will and He will take care of you." She whispered her mother's words over and over. "How is it that God would allow a mother to lose a child? Isn't having a child doing God's will?" she asked herself.

When she taught catechism to the children, she saw Emelie sitting there, in the front row. When the students asked her about death, she told them that God comes to get the good children first because He needs them most of all. She also told them that heaven was filled with good children.

Father Richard often visited with Eliza after her catechism class. Normally, she could be found under the oak, waiting for Oscar to arrive and take her home. This day was different however, and Father Richard found her standing in the doorway that led to the church rectory.

"Do you want to talk Eliza?" he asked.

"I wish I could see Emelie one more time," she replied. "I want to ask her if she is all right now. I want her to know I prayed for her to get well."

"You must have faith that she is happy," Father Richard said. "That should give you some comfort. When do you and Oscar plan to be married?"

"He hasn't really asked me yet."

"Do you want to marry now?"

"Yes, I do, but at the same time I am afraid," she said. "You don't think it's too soon, do you? After Emilie's death?" Her eyes filled with tears and she turned away.

Father Richard turned Eliza's face toward him. "You do not need to punish yourself, Eliza," he said. "Life is for the living."

She took a deep breath as she saw Oscar walking to meet her. "Thank you, Father," she whispered as she left.

Oscar looked carefully at Eliza as he helped her into the surrey. "You are sad," he said. "What has happened?"

"Father Richard asked me when we planned to be married," she replied.

"Eliza, I want to ask your family very soon for your hand," Oscar said.

"But I'm afraid. I'm really afraid," Eliza cried out.

"Of what?"

Eliza looked at Oscar. "Of dying, and afraid of living too, I guess."

"But you must think about now, not what might happen in the future. Little Regina needs you, and so do I."

"I love you," she said, "and I am certain I could love little Regina. But will that be enough?"

There was something about the air that late afternoon. Spring was near. The azaleas and camellias covered the ground with petals of pink and white, purple, red and fuchsia. The nights were still cold, but the days were filled with warm sunlight. Fuzzy tassels laced the limbs of the oak, and all the trees were busy exchanging bare branches for bright green leaves. The purple and white flowers of the Japanese magnolias looked as though someone had tied them to the bare limbs with a piece of invisible thread. The dogwood had also budded and soon the blossoms, each marked with the Crucifixion, would fill the blue skies.

Jumping the broomstick

The day finally came, on an April afternoon, when Oscar decided to ask for Eliza's hand in marriage. "I'm certain I can make your daughter happy," he told Charles Landry. "She and I have discussed the marriage, and I believe she is ready to accept me. I am asking for permission, sir, to marry Eliza."

Then Oscar turned and faced Idea. "Please accept my proposal of marriage, Madam Landry."

"We knew this time would soon come," Idea said. "You seem to be a good man, but you must realize we want only Eliza's happiness. Forgive us if we seem reluctant to accept."

Clearing his throat and holding on to his coat lapels, Charles asked, "When do you want the ceremony?"

"I hoped in a month, after the banns of marriage have been properly read."

Idea walked over to her husband. Charles put his arm around his wife's shoulder, and looked at Oscar carefully. "You have our permission, Mr. Daigle. But, if you hurt her in any way, I will personally beat you to a pulp."

Idea chuckled, and shook her head. "You must ask Eliza now, and then the children. We all must agree."

Oscar nodded, and left to find Eliza. Before she could say anything, he kissed her hand, and said, "Marry me, Eliza."

She had never seen him so serious, not even in church, and she had to remind herself that this man would soon be her husband. "Where will we live?" she asked.

"You have not been out to my land, Eliza. The house is almost finished. Our home will be waiting for us when we marry."

"And little Regina?"

"She is too little now to know what a good mother I am giving to her," Oscar pronounced. "But in time she will realize that you are the mother she never had."

Eliza's sisters and brothers were agreeable, and in fact were expecting the proposal since they had been told by Pierre that they must all say yes, or he would personally beat each one of them to a pulp in the fine Landry tradition.

That night, after everyone was in bed Idea knocked softly on the girls' bedroom door. "Eliza," she whispered, "I would like to speak to you."

"What is wrong, Mama?" Eliza asked, as she and her mother walked to the parlor.

Idea studied her daughter carefully. "My darling daughter, is this marriage really what you want?"

Eliza's eyes grew wide. "I thought you and Papa liked Oscar!"

"We do like him," Idea replied, "but we do not think you will be happy living on a plantation with freed slaves. You were not raised this way. On the contrary, you were taught to keep yourself apart from these people. Besides, do you realize you will be living in a house in the middle of nowhere?"

"But Mama! I don't feel this will be a problem. I know Oscar would not put me in a place which would make me unhappy. On the contrary, he built the house for me. The plantation has to have workers and from what Oscar tells me these are good loyal people who work hard for him. What is wrong with that?"

"There is nothing wrong with that," Idea said, "but it is not right for you."

Eliza looked at her mother. "That is my decision," she said firmly, "not yours."

~ ~ ~ ~

Mr. Gabriel Oscar Daigle married Miss Eliza Landry on the fourth Saturday of May, at two o'clock in the afternoon, in 1893. Leocade Daigle had insisted they marry in the Chapel of Saint John. "It's the proper thing to do," she told Oscar. "We are leaders here, and we must set an example."

The place of the wedding mattered little to Eliza, and she told Oscar they were going to be just as married whether the ceremony was in church or beneath the widespread arms of a big oak tree. She also told him no one really cared about the wedding ceremony because everyone was anticipating the grand party which her parents would give in their home after the wedding.

On the morning of the wedding, Charles Landry carefully laid the family broomstick across the floor at the front door. He told Eliza that she and Oscar would be expected to jump that broomstick, or their vows would not be valid. By the time the newlyweds arrived at the Landry home, most of the guests were already there and the broomstick was plainly visible through the open door.

Eliza looked at Oscar and began to laugh. "Do you think you can jump that?" she whispered as they started up the walk to the house. Grabbing his hand, Eliza took a big jump across the broomstick, pulling Oscar after her through the open door. The fiddlers played a waltz, and the newlyweds began to dance, inviting everyone to join them.

Eliza had been warned that young men would interrupt her dances by pinning money to her dress in exchange for a kiss and a chance to dance with her. At first she liked the attention, but her chances to dance with her husband began to dwindle as all the men, young and old, lined up around the parlor wall. Charles Landry saw the look on his daughter's face, and raising his hand he motioned for the fiddlers to stop the music.

"I want to thank all of you for coming to this momentous event," he said. "You have been most generous to bring such fine gifts and beautiful cakes. And there are so many chickens running loose around here that I am afraid the rooster will die from exhaustion." When the laughter subsided, he continued.

"There comes a time in every father's life when he must admit he has finished his job. He has grown old, along with his loving wife, and the times they have shared with their babies have turned into memories. The daughter is now a woman. The son is now a man. And all the wishes in the world cannot erase the hand of time. When a father gives away his daughter, he also accepts a son, and makes room in his heart for what will follow. I ask God to bless this young couple and keep their hearts filled with promise.

"And now, I want to propose a toast. Raise your glasses, all of you, and toast Mr. and Mrs. Oscar Daigle, and join with me in wishing that they live long and share many happy days together, filled with children, a reasonable amount of wealth, and a strong and steadfast faith in God."

As the guests lifted their glasses, the sun was setting, casting long shadows across the wide porch. The light filled the parlor and crept down the hallway into the dining room, turning the crisp white tablecloths pink and gold. Bottles of wine waited unopened on the sideboard. Large bowls of gumbo, grillades, and rice sat on one end of the long cypress table. In the center were platters of roast pork, boudin, and baskets of gratons. Cakes of every description and size sat on the other end.

Oscar walked into the dining room. He knew Eliza would be dancing again by now, so he filled his plate, poured a glass of wine, and sat by the window looking out over the wide gardens and majestic oaks behind the Landry home.

I can give her as much as this and more, he thought. Tonight we will be with my mother and little Regina. Tomorrow I will bring Eliza and Regina to our new home.

~ ~ ~ ~

It was almost dark when the fringed surrey arrived with the bride and groom at the Daigle home. Oscar told Eliza, "My father was always very proud of his position as Senator. My brothers and I were never allowed to do much because he was afraid we would misbehave and disgrace the family name. In fact," he added, "the name Daigle means 'of eagles' and we were taught we must respect that name until we die." Eliza remembered those words as she walked up the steps which led to the front gallery. Leocade opened the door to the newlyweds with Regina sleeping in her arms.

"Hello, my darling," she said to Eliza. "Come in. You must be exhausted." She looked at Regina, and then at Eliza. "Would you like to hold your daughter?"

Eliza took the baby into her arms. Regina wiggled a little, then opened her eyes and looked at her new mother as Eliza pressed her lips against her tiny head.

"Oh, Oscar," she whispered. "She is so beautiful."

"Yes, she is," he answered. "And so are you."

"The cradle is next to the bed in the front room," Leocade said as she walked to the upstairs bedroom. "It will be quiet up here. Regina should sleep all night."

Eliza could tell this was the finest bedroom in the house. The windows were covered in silk and matched the bed's comforter which touched the floor. Two little steps on each side of the bed were covered in matching silk, and the baby's cradle was draped with a fine netting which reflected the light from the lanterns. On both sides of the room were matching mirrored chests, one for the lady and one for the gentleman. The drawers were decorated with ivory pulls and silk tassels. A lavatory sat under one window with a crystal pitcher filled with water. Beside the pitcher was a crystal dish with pale green soap and crisp cotton cloths, neatly folded to show an embroidered "D".

"I will bring you something to eat," Leocade said and then turned quickly at the sound of something hitting one of the front bedroom windows.

"What was that?" Eliza asked.

When Oscar looked out the window he saw his brothers leading a large group of friends through the front yard. As the men walked, they were beating large pots with spoons and throwing stones against the house.

"Oh, Oscar," Leocade laughed, "they have all come to congratulate the old man who has married the young maiden. They are not likely to go away easily!"

Oscar shook his head. "I can't have this on my wedding night. We are tired, and this racket will wake Regina!"

"What do you want?" he called to the mob already filling the downstairs. "You are trespassing. Go away."

"We want to congratulate you, old man!" they cried in unison. "You are a lucky man. Come down so we can show you how much we like you!"

"What will it take for you to leave us alone?"

"Some food. And a lot of drink!"

"Mama," Oscar called out. "Give my friends a lot to drink, and a little food."

Several hours passed before the house was quiet once again. Eliza opened her eyes. The room was dark, save one small lantern on the gentleman's chest. She saw her husband leaning over her, his white shirt outlined in dancing gold light. She turned and looked at the baby sleeping, her little lips curled and wet. What peace, she thought. I am at home with eagles.

~ ~ ~ ~

The late morning sky was filled with clouds. Oscar awoke and turned to look at Eliza lying next to him, almost lost in the down pillows and comforter. He studied her face. He loved her eyes, but she was beautiful even when her eyes were closed. She moved slightly and then drifted off to sleep again. He touched the ring he had placed on her finger a few hours before. He slipped his hand in hers. How small and young she was, only seventeen. The sound of thunder and the rain hitting the windows woke Eliza, and she looked at her husband and smiled.

"Hello, my grand eagle," she whispered. "Has the smallest eagle returned yet?"

Oscar saw that Regina's cradle was empty. "Who came to get her?" Oscar asked. "Mama?"

"No," Eliza said, "it was your brother Francois."

"Who?" Oscar asked. "Francois? Can't be!"

Oscar and Eliza came downstairs quickly and found Francois showing Regina the raindrops on the breakfast room window pane.

Oscar looked at him and shook his head in disbelief. "What is this? You, holding a baby? Since when?"

Francois laughed. "And why not? What better pastime for the son of a politician with the same name?"

"And kissing a baby too," Eliza chimed in.

"Since when are you a politician?" Oscar asked.

"Aw, come on, big brother. You know I am the one most like Papa."

Francois bent over Regina and kissed her head. "There! I have done my fair share of hugging and kissing. Now Regina, I'm giving you to your mother." He handed the baby to Eliza, and stroking his mustache walked quickly into the parlor and closed the door.

"Oscar, when can we leave for our home?" Eliza asked, glancing out the window. The rain had stopped, and long fingers of sunlight were slicing the clouds apart.

"As soon as you and Regina are ready," he answered.

Journey to Eagle Crest

The miles between the Daigle home and Oscar's plantation slowly disappeared. Eliza tried to imagine what her life would be like now. She stroked the baby asleep in her arms. Regina looked like Oscar, with dark hair and blue eyes. Will she have a bed ready in our new house? Eliza wondered. How many children will Oscar and I have? Will they look like me?

"What is our house like?" she asked Oscar.

"Cher, I think you will like the house. I built it for you. Of course, I had help from my men who work the plantation. You will meet them all soon, and you will see."

The countryside began to change. Houses with wide lawns were replaced by fields of crops. In the distance Eliza could see the ripples that the wind was making in the young sugar cane. When Oscar pulled the surrey up to the front of the house, Eliza sat very still. He looked at her and asked, "Well, what do you think about this?"

"I never dreamed it would be like this," she said. "It seems too big for three people, and the land! It stretches for miles and miles. Is all this yours?"

"Ours!" Oscar laughed. "There is more that I will build. We need a potato shed. The orchards must be fenced, and I think the smokehouse is too small for a big family. But first you must see all of it, and meet my friends."

Eliza walked up the front steps and stopped on the porch. Her heart was beating so fast that she was certain Oscar could hear it. Opening the door, she walked into a large room with windows which looked out on the front porch. There was a fireplace, and a few chairs, and at one end there was a bed with a small table next to it, and a cradle.

"Is this the parlor?" she asked.

"Yes," Oscar answered, "and it is also our room." Through a doorway to the left there was another room. "This is a bedroom," he said, "maybe for the boys. And the room behind our room would be best for the girls, I think. They need to be close to us."

"And what about the room behind the boy's room?" Eliza asked.

33

"That can be another bedroom. There is a door which leads to the outside. A guest room, perhaps?"

Souri

By now Eliza was in the kitchen, which stretched all across the back of the house, with an outside door on either end. There was a large table with benches and chairs, a wood burning stove, and several large crocks filled with food. Along one of the walls was a table with a wash basin. Standing in front of the basin was a young girl with skin so black it glistened like wet onyx.

"Eliza, I want you to meet Souri. Her father is my friend and the one who takes care of everything here. She will help you with the house and the cooking."

"Hello, Souri," Eliza said, walking over to the girl. "I'm certainly glad to see you!"

Souri laughed. "Don't worry, Miss Eliza. I know how to do lots of things. And Mr. Oscar thinks I'm a good cook, too." She watched out the back window as Oscar took Eliza's arm and led her past the smokehouse and the chicken and pig yards to the barn. Souri could see Oscar gesturing toward the pasture, and she thought he was probably explaining to Eliza where the pond was. "I sure hope that man doesn't scare Miss Eliza away with all that talk about chickens and pigs and barns and ponds filled with fish and crawfish," she whispered. "Lord, that could kill her dead right on the spot!"

When Eliza returned to the house, she told Oscar, "I feel so little, so young. Why, even Souri knows more than I do. How long will it take for me to learn how to do things here?"

"A very short time with help from me and Souri," Oscar replied.

"Miss Eliza," Souri said, "tomorrow my father will bring the chest he has made for you and we will unpack your things then." Souri was carrying a pitcher filled with water and a metal basin which she placed on the table in the front room. From the pocket of her apron, she pulled a large bar of white soap and laid it next to the basin. "My Mama made some special towels for you," she said. "I'll go home and get them."

"Where do you live?" Eliza asked.

Souri walked to the front window. "See that little house way over there past the big oak? That's my house. I live there with my Mama and my Pappy and my two little sisters."

Eliza looked in the direction of Souri's house. There were other houses there also, lined up in a row. They all looked the same, like little boxes with a door and windows. Souri's house was the only one with a porch.

"Are there others in your family?" she asked.

"I have two brothers. One works here, but he has his own house because he used to be married and has a little boy. My other brother works in the town, and helps my Pappy when the crops come in."

"Where does he live?" Eliza asked.

"He lives with my aunt, NaNoot. You will meet her when you have babies, Miss Eliza."

The sun had slipped below the horizon, and for miles the sky was pink and gold, and deep blue. Eliza held Regina up to the window and watched as Souri walked past the old oak which grew next to the house. Chickens were beginning to roost in its branches, nestling like ornaments in the green leaves. Just past the oak was the

35

orchard, its trees heavy with oranges and pears. Oscar said there would soon be peaches and in the fall, pecans. Eliza could see grape vines growing along the fence which surrounded the house. She wondered whether the grapes would be as sweet as those which grew wild in Côte Gelée.

When Souri returned with the towels, lights had already appeared in the windows of the little houses. Oscar was bringing a ham in from the smokehouse when Souri and Eliza walked into the kitchen.

"Here, Papa Daigle," Eliza said, "take your daughter and give her some milk. Souri and I will fix supper."

The two women worked side by side, slicing ham and bread, and coring pears, which Souri poached in sugar and water on the stove. After her milk, Regina fell asleep and Souri took her. Eliza sat at the kitchen table on one of the benches. There was a sense of calm which filled the house, and she thought about all the servants her mother had. Not one of them had ever spoken to her like a friend. Oscar opened a bottle of wine, and he and Eliza ate supper.

CHAPTER THREE

"ELIZA! ELIZA! WHERE are you, girl?"

The sun was already up, and Eliza awoke with a start. "Who is that?" she whispered. "That voice. That's someone I know!" Oscar was gone and Regina was still asleep in her cradle. Eliza heard Souri's voice coming from the porch.

"Miss Eliza's asleep, thank you for asking! Who are you?"

"I am the person in charge of making certain Miss Eliza, as you call her, is happy and safe way out here in the middle of nowhere."

"Oh, no," Eliza gasped. "That is Pierre!" She jumped out of bed and ran to the window. "What are you doing here?" she asked. "And why isn't Mama or Papa with you?"

"Because," Pierre said, "I am perfectly capable of telling the horse what to do."

"Oh, really?" she answered. "Since when?"

"Since you left and my life changed for the better! Besides I have several messages from home."

"And what are they, may I ask?"

"The first message is from Helen. She wants to know if she can have your bed now. The second message is from Mama. She wants to know when you are coming to get the rest of your stuff."

"Tell Helen she can have the bed. I don't care about it anymore. Tell Mama I will come for the rest of my stuff when Souri's father brings me the chest he has made for me."

"Souri?"

"Yes. Souri. You have a problem with that?"

"Do you know what that name means?" Pierre was grinning and rocking on his heels.

"Yes, I do," Eliza sniffed. "It means mouse. And she is just like a tiny mouse – a nice mouse at that."

"I'm not impressed," Pierre replied.

"You don't impress me either," Eliza answered quickly. "Besides all that, would you like to come inside, and see my new home?"

Pierre grinned again, and asked, "Got any food?"

Souri was already busy preparing breakfast when Pierre and Eliza walked into the kitchen. "This is my brother," Eliza said. "He will be joining me."

"Yes, Miss Eliza," Souri answered as she pulled a tray of cornbread out of the oven. "Here, y'all can get started on this!" Eliza watched Pierre as he cut three pieces of cornbread and covered them with cane syrup.

"Where is your husband?" Pierre asked, with his mouth full.

"I don't know," Eliza answered.

"Maybe he has had enough already!" Pierre snickered.

"Souri!" Eliza asked, "Where is Oscar?"

"He's by the pond, Miss Eliza. He said something about a whole lot of crawfish waiting to be caught."

Eliza and Pierre walked past the barn to the edge of one of the cotton fields where the pond sat, surrounded by tall grass and trees. Oscar was leading a horse hooked to a seine net around the pond. Thick brown waves swirled across the net, making slapping sounds in the mud along the banks. He stopped to rake the crawfish into one of the cotton sacks when he spied Eliza. He quickly tied the sack shut, and walking to his wife, he picked her up and swung her around.

"Good morning, Mrs. Daigle," he sang. "How did you sleep?"

"Very well, thank you," she sang.

"I slept well too," sang Pierre.

"Well, well, hello my man," Oscar said as he shook Pierre's hand. "What brings you here to Eagle Crest?"

"Eagle Crest?" Eliza asked. "When did you name the plantation Eagle Crest?"

"Just now," Oscar replied. "I was fishing in the pond and trying to think of a name for our new home. Then it came to me. It is what our name means. I think it is perfect, don't you?"

"I think it is perfect too," Pierre said, smiling at Oscar.

Eliza glared at her brother. "What are you really doing here, Pierre?" she asked. "I know you did not come all this way to give me two messages."

"You are right," Pierre said. "I have some news. Mama is going to have another baby."

"Are you sure?" Eliza asked in a tone which showed how little she believed her brother. "Why didn't Mama tell me herself?"

"Well, in the first place, she suspected this right before you got married, but she didn't want people to think about her instead of you." Pierre's eyes were wide as he spoke, and Eliza became concerned.

"How does she feel?"

"So so, I guess," Pierre answered, shrugging his shoulders. "How do women feel during all this anyway? She says the baby will probably be born sometime early next year, like January maybe."

Eliza looked at Oscar. "This is probably a good thing, don't you think? Mama has not been happy since Emelie died. A new baby might help."

Joseph

Oscar carried the sack of wiggling crawfish as he and Eliza walked with Pierre back to the house. When they were halfway, Souri's father, Joseph met them, and taking the sack from Oscar, he carried it to the well and doused the crawfish with water before bringing the sack into the kitchen.

"Joe, tell Souri to start a pot of water to boil," Oscar said. "And, by the way, where is the chest you made for Eliza?"

"I'll get it, Mr. Oscar," Joseph answered as he turned around and walked back towards the row of tiny houses in the distance.

After Pierre left, Oscar and Souri boiled the crawfish and Eliza waited at the window for Joseph to return. As he approached, Eliza could see that he was a strong man. He easily carried the chest on his shoulder, making the veins in his muscular arms stand out against his dark, shiny skin. Souri does not look like him, Eliza thought. She opened the door as he brought the chest inside. Regina had just begun to crawl, and was making her way across the parlor floor.

"Here you are, Miss Eliza," Joseph said as he set the chest beside the bed and went to pick up Regina. The baby let out a shriek and he laughed. "All babies do that when they see me, even the old ones!" Joseph looked around at the inside of the house. "What do you think of the house Mr. Oscar has built for you?" he asked.

"It is a wonderful house, Joseph," she answered. "There is so much inside and outside to make anyone happy."

"Miss Eliza," Joseph said, "you will become part of this land, you and all your babies, because land is the only real thing there is. You will be just like me and my family. Mr. Oscar's mama was given this land because her pappy was a lieutenant in the Civil War. Way back then, my grandparents were slaves and they worked this land. When Mr. Oscar's mama gave this land to her children, we stayed because this is where we belong. The land will take care of you, feed you and make clothes for you. It will give you money after it makes you work hard, just like a mama does. It will teach you how to live. And, when you die the land will cover you up so that you can sleep. My mammy and pappy are buried just about halfway between this house and my house, in that big wide space past that old oak tree. Every time I walk across that spot, I remember that the land will come to cover us all."

"I don't see any crosses or markers, Joseph," Eliza said.

"That's right, Miss Eliza, there ain't none. We are still slaves, and slaves are buried in unmarked graves."

"Why do you say you are still slaves? I thought all slaves had been set free."

"Aren't you always a child to your mama and daddy? In the same way, we are always slaves to our masters."

Oscar appeared in the doorway to the kitchen and announced the crawfish were ready. Eliza looked up at her husband as though she had been awakened from a deep sleep. "I'm coming," she answered. "I'm coming."

The steam from the deep red crawfish rose in small clouds from the big bowl placed in the center of the table. "Y'all wait until they cool a bit," Souri said. "Miss Regina acts like she wants some. Look at the way she's trying to climb up onto the bench with her mama. Come here, little one," she whispered as she picked the baby up and squeezed her. "Time for a nap."

Oscar studied Eliza's face as she sat across from him in the kitchen. "Is something bothering you, Cher?" he asked.

41

"No, it's just that Joseph gave me a lot to think about."

"I saw you talking with him. What did he say?"

"So many things that I think are important to remember. For example, he said he will always be a slave even though he is free now."

"Yes, I know. He has told that to me in those same words. He is, in many ways, a very smart man, and he understands a lot about the way things really are in life. But, on the other hand, he can be very dramatic. I think it is because he likes the attention."

"Perhaps," Eliza said. "I don't know enough about life here to know if he is right or not."

"Did he tell you about the graveyard?"

"Yes. Do you know if it is true?"

"I think it probably is true because I have heard that story since I was a little boy. I remember my brothers and I wanted to dig a hole out there just to see if we could find a dead slave."

"Oh, good Lord," Eliza cried. "I think we should just eat our crawfish and not discuss this anymore!"

CHAPTER FOUR

LIFE AT EAGLE Crest began to fill each crevice of Eliza's being, and soon Côte Gelée began to fade, like the colors in an old dress. Eliza and Souri became friends, and although it seemed natural that Eliza would become the teacher and Souri the student, it was actually the reverse. Soon Eliza was asking Souri what it felt like to milk a cow.

"Why, Miss Eliza, you never milked a cow?" Souri gasped.

"No," Eliza answered. "My father didn't allow his daughters to do such things. But, you know, Souri, I always wondered about that."

"I can tell you all about milking!" Souri laughed. "First thing, is make sure your hands are warm before you milk those cows!"

"Do you really think that makes a difference?" Eliza asked.

"Why yes, it does," Souri answered. "A cow can tell if you want her to give milk by the way your hands feel. If they are too cold, then the cow says, no thank you, not today!"

Eliza giggled. "Then what?"

"I could show you real good if I had a milking stool. You wait here, and I'll go and get one, or would you like to come to the barn and meet Petunia?"

"I think I'd like to meet Petunia," Eliza answered.

Inside the barn Petunia waited patiently. Souri motioned to the milking stool and said, "Now Miss Eliza, I'll just sit down here, real calm like, and rub my hands together to make them warm like I said."

43

Souri closed her hands around two teats and made tugging motions. "You have to start milking right away, or she might go to sleep," Souri whispered. The milk came in short spurts squirting into the bucket. "Pretty soon this bucket is gonna be full. We should be able to catch some cream off the top. Would you like to make some butter?"

Souri showed Eliza how to catch the cream and put it into a bottle, and then shake the bottle until it turned into pale yellow butter. Then Souri baked some bread and the two of them sat there at the big table and watched the butter disappear into each slice.

"How did Souri get to be so smart?" Eliza asked Oscar.

"All the black women on the plantation are smart, just like Souri," he answered. "Their mamas taught them how to do everything. Their mamas knew how to do all these things because when they were little girls they worked as slaves for white women just like you. When the slaves were set free, the black women stayed, and most of them continued to work for the white women because they wanted to and sometimes because they had no other place to go."

~ ~ ~ ~

Spring was turning quickly into summer. The corn was dry enough to go to the mill now, and Oscar planned to stop there when he took Eliza to Côte Gelée to visit her parents. The heat had already bleached the trees dusty green and made the narrow dirt roads to Côte Gelée dry like brown powder. Stores lined Pinhook Road on either side. When Oscar pointed to the different shops, Eliza was amazed.

"I didn't know all this was here," she said.

Oscar laughed. "You will probably visit these shops often now. That is what happens when you marry and have a house to care for."

Up ahead, Eliza could see the fine homes of the rich people sitting high on the banks of the Vermilion River. Oscar suddenly pointed to one of the houses.

"Cher, look on the right at that big house with the bell in the front. Next to that house is the mill. We'll bring our corn there."

"That bell looks just like the bell Mama has next to the kitchen door," Eliza said. "I wonder if they use it to call everyone to dinner like Mama does."

By the time Oscar and Eliza crossed the Pinhook Bridge, the Vermilion Queen was already docked, and the sun was low in the sky.

"Oh, Oscar, look at the big boat!" Eliza cried. "How pretty she is!"

"Perhaps we can take a ride on her, Cher," he answered. "I think we could even take Regina."

This was Eliza's favorite time of the day when the countryside seemed to yawn and slowly fall asleep with the sun. A lone white egret flew across the gold and pink clouds, his feathers blushing in the sunlight. Crickets were singing and oil lamps began to appear in windows as the surrey pulled into the front yard of Charles and Idea Landry. Eliza felt her heart in her throat, and somewhere in her mind were images of a little girl playing on the porch. Before Oscar was able to help Eliza out of the surrey, Idea and Charles grabbed their daughter's hand and pulled her down into their arms. Idea brushed Eliza's hair out of her face.

"It has been only a few weeks since the wedding, and it seems like an eternity!" she said.

"Mama, are you feeling all right?" Eliza asked, looking closely at Idea.

"Well, I am feeling good, Eliza. But where is little Regina?"

"Oscar felt it would be too long a trip for her," Eliza answered, "so we left her with Souri. Where are the others?"

"Alcide is with Pierre and Edmond. They are all spending the night in Lafayette helping Father Richard, and Helen and Marie are asleep in your old bed."

Eliza shut her eyes and she could hear the sound of people talking about the weather. She heard children playing, and she was a young girl again.

Idea broke the silence. "Eliza, tell me how is married life?"

Eliza looked at her mother. Idea had grown grey somehow, and her skin was not as smooth as it had been. The kerosene lamp cast a yellow light around the room making the shadows on her face dance.

"I'm fine, Mama," Eliza replied. "I have Souri to help me, and Regina is growing everyday!"

"Is Souri Joseph's daughter?" Idea asked.

"Yes! Do you know the family?"

"Joseph has worked for the Daigle family for many, many years. His sister is a midwife, NaNoot à les Yeux Vert. She was here when you were born."

"I think Souri mentioned that name," Eliza said. "I suppose she has green eyes, right? Will NaNoot be here for the birth of your baby?"

"Most certainly," Idea replied.

"Where are you ladies hiding, eh?" Charles called out as he and Oscar walked onto the porch. "We need to treat our guests to a late supper, if they are hungry, or at least to a late drink!"

"Are you hungry?" Idea asked Eliza.

"Yes, Mama," Eliza answered, "very hungry, for some strange reason!"

"That is because you are home," Charles said, "and someone else has fixed the food. It always tastes better that way."

When the evening was finished, Eliza kissed her parents good night as she had done many nights before, and turned to walk down the hall toward her old bedroom.

"Remember you will have to sleep in the spare bedroom," Idea said. "Your sisters won't let you back into your old room; I'm sure of that!"

"I know, Mama," Eliza answered. "I just want to see how they look in my bed."

Eliza gently opened the door. Marie's face was covered with the edge of the sheet so that all that was visible was her forehead and one eye. Helen was lying on her back, and Eliza could hear her breathing in the stillness.

"Where is the spare bedroom?" Oscar asked.

"Through the kitchen," Eliza replied. "The door is on the right. It's the room most people call the stranger's room, like the room we have at Eagle Crest."

Oscar opened the door to the tiny bedroom and walked in. There was a bed against the wall, a small chest, and one chair with a seat made from horsehair. Over the chest was a small window. The fruit orchard was visible through the window in the moonlight. Eliza looked around the room, and sitting on the bed she bounced up and down.

"Moss," she said.

"All beds have moss, right?" Oscar asked.

47

Eliza punched the mattress down with her fist. "I'm not sure. It could be moss or horsehair, or a combination. What do you think?"

"I think we should go to bed." Oscar whispered.

Once they had settled down between the thick cotton sheets, Eliza quipped, "Moss for sure! Do you know how this room got its name?"

"No, but I'm sure I will have to stay awake to hear?" her husband answered, bunching the pillow up under his head and folding his hands across his chest.

"Well," Eliza began. Oscar sighed. "Don't do that," she snapped back. "You are distracting me."

"Go on, Mrs. Daigle," he whispered.

"Long ago people couldn't have a guest room for people they hardly knew. You know, most strangers can't be trusted."

"I don't think that is always true," Oscar answered.

"Maybe not always," Eliza said, "but most of the time. People decided to build a separate room on their houses and call it the stranger's room. The room was usually situated next to the kitchen and had a door leading to the outside. This way the stranger could come and go without disturbing the family. And," she said, taking a deep breath, "the family could lock the kitchen door and keep the stranger out completely if someone was afraid, or there was a serious problem."

"Like what?" Oscar asked, turning to look at his wife buried in the down pillows. "Aren't you a little dramatic?"

"Maybe just a little," Eliza sniffed. "But bad things sometimes happen when strangers are allowed to run lose all over the place."

"Good night, Cher!" Oscar said as he extinguished the oil lamp.

~ ~ ~ ~

"Come have breakfast with us!" Idea called through the closed door. Eliza could hear Helen and Marie giggling in the kitchen. "Hush," one of the girls said. "No, you hush loudmouth!" the other replied.

Oscar opened the door with such force the girls ran shrieking into the kitchen. "Well, well," he said, "I see you have decided to get up early for a change!" Helen and Marie walked up to Oscar, and kissing him on the cheek they said, "Good morning, dear brother-in-law."

By the time breakfast was over, all of Eliza's clothes were in the surrey, and Oscar was pacing back and forth in the parlor. Idea opened the door to a bookcase and pulled out a small Bible.

"Eliza," she said, "my mother gave this to me when I first married your father. It was, for the longest time the only book I read. I want you to take it."

The Pinhook Bridge joined Côte Gelée with Lafayette and became visible as Oscar and Eliza approached the city. The Vermilion Queen had already left on her daily visits to the small towns along the Vermilion River. Eliza could see a line of buggies waiting at the mill on the river bank.

"Did you know there are homes in the city that have telephones now?" Oscar asked his wife.

"Telephones!" Eliza said. "Who has a telephone?"

"The man who will grind our corn," Oscar answered. "I was here two weeks ago, and I talked on it." Oscar pulled the surrey into the line of buggies. "I think the telephone is a luxury of the rich, at least for now. I'm not sure we will ever have a telephone as long as we live in the country."

"How does it work?" she asked.

"The voices travel along wires like the words in a telegraph," Oscar said. "Would you like to see my friend's telephone?"

"No, not now," Eliza replied, "I'm too tired." After all, she thought, I can barely absorb being married and moving away from home.

Eliza noticed other mills along the river banks. There were logs floating down the river as she and Oscar rode over the bridge, and she assumed what she saw on the left was a saw mill. Across from the saw mill was the restaurant she had heard so much about.

"If we stopped to eat at that restaurant, what would we eat?" Eliza asked Oscar.

"Probably fried chicken," he answered. "That's what they are famous for. Why? Are you hungry?"

"No," Eliza said. "I wanted to know if you knew how the bridge got its name."

Sensing another stranger's room conversation, Oscar replied, "No, do you?"

Eliza looked at her husband. "Well, if you are really interested, the story goes something like this," she said. "The owner of the restaurant stuck a grain of corn on a pin bent like hook. He tied the hook to a piece of string and threw it out of the restaurant's window, and tried to catch the neighbor's chickens to fry for lunch."

"Obviously he was successful," Oscar interjected. "The fried chicken is the best in Lafayette. Nice and tender with a faint taste of corn."

Eliza looked steadily ahead, and never acknowledged her husband's attempt to make fun of her story once again. By the time they reached Eagle Crest, it was past twelve noon, and Eliza knew Regina would be asleep. "Souri," she called out. "Souri, we are here!"

There was no answer as they walked through the front door. The crib was empty and Regina and Souri were nowhere to be found. Then Eliza heard a familiar shriek, and looking out the window, she saw Regina and Souri running behind baby chicks in the yard. Regina was barefoot in the dust, and a ring of brown dirt circled her lips. She was squealing and laughing as the chicks ran one way and then the other.

"Oh, no!" Eliza gasped. But then she caught herself, and began to laugh. "Where is the baby I bathed yesterday?" she called out. Souri looked up, and grabbing Regina, she wiped her face with her apron. As Eliza hugged Regina, she saw a small black woman standing under the oak. "Who is that?" she asked.

Isabel

"Why, that's my momma, Miss Eliza!"

"What's her name?"

"Isabel," Souri answered, smiling. "She wanted to meet you in person, up close. That's why she's waiting."

"Tell her to come, Souri. She looks more like your sister than your momma." Eliza was amazed at the resemblance. Both were small. Both had skin as black as night. Both were pretty like the women in a picture she once saw of island people. The three women talked about Oscar and Regina and the plantation. When Isabel left, Eliza felt a strange sensation, as though she was disloyal to her own mother. Why don't I see a difference between myself and these people? she wondered.

51

"Momma!" Souri called. "Today is the day you promised to help me and Miss Eliza."

"I hear you child," Isabel answered. "I haven't forgotten. Go on back now and tell Miss Eliza I'm coming soon as I finish my dishes."

Isabel watched her oldest daughter walk back to Oscar's house. Her hands rested in a washtub full of breakfast dishes and soap bubbles. She had been Joseph's wife for a hundred years, it seemed. There had been six babies, three girls and three boys. One of the boys died from yellow fever when he was three years old. The rest of the children all stayed on the plantation and helped their pappy except for Lucius. He lived some of the time with Joseph's sister, NaNoot.

"That child!" Isabel said to herself, as Souri disappeared into Oscar's house. "If only she could have a chance at something else sides this." She stared into the washtub, swirling the soapy water with one finger. "I just want her to have more."

"Miss Eliza, she's coming," Souri said, walking into the kitchen where Eliza was cutting up large pieces of beef. For several weeks now, Souri had been helping Eliza prepare the noon meal for the workers. Summer was drawing to a close, harvest time was near, and the number of people needing to be fed had increased to well over thirty men, women, and children. Isabel and Joseph were experts at feeding large groups of workers. They had been doing that for fifty years.

Oscar remembered his mother saying, "All you have to do is take care of your workers, and they will take care of you." He had fixed many meals for his workers before he married Eliza. When Souri became old enough she helped, but it was Isabel who could fill the plates high with meat and gravy and potatoes. Her cornbread made the men cry out with joy, and her sweet potatoes baked in cane syrup would stop a fight if need be.

As soon as Isabel arrived, she began to peel and slice the potatoes and carrots, quickly filling three large basins by the time the smell of beef simmered with sliced onions drifted slowly out the kitchen windows. Outside the windows the workers were gathering, drawn by the smell of stew and fresh bread.

One worker whistled and said, "Man! Don't that smell good!"

Another worker called out, "Miss Isabel, can we have some molasses to help us finish off that bread?"

The light coming through the kitchen windows suddenly grew dim. The sky turned dark, and clouds hung heavy across the tops of the trees. The wind began to blow straight from the south and the whistling sounds it made caused Eliza to shiver. She never liked bad weather, especially in the summer time, when the air was so hot it took your breath away.

"We had better hurry and fill the plates before the rain starts," she said. "The workers need time to get to the barn and eat."

The rain lashed at the windows as gusts of wind rattled the doors and made the shutters flap against the house. Little drops of water ran down the inside of the door and onto the kitchen floor. Eliza folded her hands and whispered prayers. In between the bursts of thunder and lightening, she heard the workers singing and laughing in the barn. Eliza remembered when she was a little girl, her mother had gathered all the children together in the center of the house during bad weather. They had prayed loudly to God and all the saints in heaven. "God will take care of us," her mother said. "He is our Father, watching over us. Pray," she whispered to her children, "pray, and you will not be afraid."

After a while, the wind stopped blowing, and the rain became a steady patter. Then the rain stopped, and the sun came out so bright that Eliza could see a rainbow high above the fields beyond the barn. The workers emerged from the barn slowly, and returned to the fields or their houses with the children or to their work on the fence which surrounded the orchard.

"Miss Eliza," Souri called out as she walked into the kitchen. "Did you see the rainbow?"

"Yes! I did. But I thought you had missed it, Souri."

"Oh, no," Souri said, "we all saw it. We always look for one when it rains like that in the middle of the day."

"That's God answering our prayers for rain," Isabel joined in. "And that rainbow is His blessing on the crops."

Oscar reached for a sack of nails on the table and turned to walk out the door. "In my case," he said, "the rain has stopped so that Joseph and I can finish the new smokehouse before the boucherie next month."

Joseph followed, carrying two hammers. Before long, the work on the smokehouse competed with the conversation in the kitchen, and Eliza left to put Regina down for a nap. Isabel looked down into a different sink of dirty dishes and swirled the soapy water with her finger once again.

"Are you happy, child?" she asked Souri.

The sound of hammering was loud now, and steady. Souri could hear only one hammer, and she knew that her father was holding the cypress boards in place so that Oscar could nail them into the frame of the smokehouse. Souri looked at her mother. Isabel seemed to be the same, but people often said she had grown old and tired. "She ain't never known anything but cooking, cleaning, and helping the white woman of the house," Souri told

54

people who said that, but she knew the real reason Isabel was growing old. It was because there would never be anything else for her. It was too late now, and Joseph needed to stay on the plantation because Eagle Crest was all he had ever known.

"Yes," Souri answered. "I'm happy."

"Why are you happy, Souri?"

"Oh, I don't know," Souri sighed. "Maybe because I don't have anything to be sad about. Are you happy?"

"I've been happier," Isabel answered.

"When was that?"

"I think it was when you all were little, and I had all my babies around me, and your pappy was young too, and strong enough to carry me."

"Did he carry me?"

"He carried all of you, all at the same time!" Isabel said, laughing. "Why, you and your sisters would hang from his strong arms like little monkeys, and your brothers would grab him around the knees, so he couldn't go anywhere."

"I remember that!" Souri squealed. "I remember he gave us candy so we would leave him alone."

"Yes, then you all grew up, and all of that changed. We changed too. We got old and we lost our chance to become something else but hired help. Why, we are no better than slaves. Now I don't mean to sound ungrateful, Souri, but it's the truth. We get paid a little money, we can grow a little garden, and maybe gather moss. That's the only difference."

"But you can leave here, and go to the city. Maybe there's work for you like Lucius found. Maybe you can do what NaNoot does. Course I'd sure miss you, but we'd get along. Sure, we could do it." Souri bit her lip and turned to look out the window.

Isabel shook her head. "And do what, child? I'm too old now except to wash dishes, take care of your sisters, and help Miss Eliza. But you could leave. You could go to the city and find good work. Look at you. You are a beautiful girl. Some fine young boy would snatch you up just like that!" And Isabel snapped her fingers.

"Why, I like it here! Mr. Oscar and Miss Eliza are good to me, and I love little Regina just like she was mine."

"I know, child. I know," Isabel said, drying her hands. "That's the problem with us. We don't know how to leave."

CHAPTER FIVE

"SADDLE MY HORSE, Samuel! Where are you, boy?"

"Right here, Mrs. D," Samuel answered. "Right here where you told me to be, next to the cistern, fixing your rows of flowers."

"Leave that alone. I want you to saddle Southern Belle," Leocade Daigle called out again.

Samuel walked out from behind the cistern. "Where you going, Mrs. D?"

"I think I'll go to visit Oscar. Lord knows I haven't had a good look at that land since I gave it to him."

Samuel B. Cross had taken care of the Daigle horses ever since the Senator died. Of course, Samuel wasn't much older than the Daigle boys when he learned to saddle the horses for the family, but he was a natural. He was little like those famous jockeys, and he could even stand up in the stirrups and, when no one was looking, ride like the wind through the pastures. But he could not rival Leocade. At least once each month, she rode across her property which stretched for miles and miles to the west, all the way to the Mermentau River.

"That road to the east is rough, Mrs. D," Samuel said. "You'd best take Mister. He's stronger."

"I know that," she shot back, glaring at the little black stable boy. "Saddle Southern Belle. She's the best riding horse around. I'd rather be comfortable than safe."

By the time Samuel brought Southern Belle around, Leocade was waiting on the porch. "What took you so long?" she asked.

"Now, Mrs. D, I just took a second or two," Samuel answered, holding the reins as Leocade pulled her long skirt to the front and tucked the hem into her belt. Taking the reins, she mounted Southern Belle and rode away at full gallop. "She never was one to take to a side saddle," Samuel mumbled.

~ ~ ~ ~

Oscar saw someone on horseback coming up to Eagle Crest, and then riding toward the houses of the workers. "Eliza," he called. "Are you expecting someone?"

"No," she answered. "Why?" She left the kitchen and stood next to Oscar. "Who do you think that is?"

Oscar raised his hand to shield his eyes from the sun, and began to laugh. "Well, there is only one person who can ride like that. It's Mama!"

"Are you sure?" Eliza asked. "Why is she going there?"

"I don't know, but she is probably going to Joseph's house," he answered as he began walking toward the workers' houses.

Oscar was already past the old oak when Eliza caught up with him. "I wish I had known your mother was coming," she said. "We really don't have a place for her to sleep."

Oscar looked at his wife and realized she was more surprised than he was. "She probably won't spend the night with us," he said. "Don't worry. If she does, I'll figure something out."

The walk to the house of Joseph and Isabel was long. Eliza wondered why they had not saddled the horses and rode the distance, but Oscar insisted it was not far enough away for that. The grass under Eliza's shoes crunched from lack of rain. This was one of the driest Septembers on record, and all around the dust blew in swirls, filling their noses with grit and making rings around their mouths and eyes.

"When am I going to get to ride Crescent?" Eliza asked her husband. The horse Oscar had bought for her was two years old now, and she had been broken for almost that long. Her mane was the color of coffee milk, and the rest of her coat was deep brown like the ground after a good rain. Between her eyes she had a white mark shaped exactly like a crescent moon.

"She is ready for you now," he said. "I rode her yesterday, and I was able to handle her with no trouble. She is not a jumper though. You can only ride for now. No tricks."

They had almost reached the house when Leocade walked onto the porch and called out, "Well, it's about time I get to see the two of you."

"Mama," Oscar said, hugging her tightly. "You are always a surprise!"

"Hello, Mama D," Eliza added, grabbing Leocade's hand. "I hope you will come to the house to see little Regina. She will be so happy."

Leocade looked at her son and his bride. They had both changed in the six months since the wedding. Oscar's face was tan, and there were little wrinkles around his blue eyes. Very becoming, she thought. Eliza seemed more beautiful, with a certain look of strength which, Leocade guessed, came from trying to live with a man like Oscar.

"I'll be by to see Regina shortly," she answered. "But first I want Joseph to ride with me to the back pasture."

"What are you looking for, Mama?"

"It looks to me like you've got a good harvest of cane, and cotton, and even some late corn back there. Are you ready?"

59

"I think so. Joseph has already assigned the workers. We should be starting this week."

"That's all well and good, but I want to see the crops before they land in the back of wagons on the way to the mill. That's the only way I can tell if you are putting the land to good use." Leocade mounted Southern Belle and looking down at Oscar, she said, "You and Joseph walk back to your house and saddle up the horses. I'll meet you there."

Eliza grabbed Oscar's hand. "Can I saddle Crescent, and meet you?" she asked.

"Visit with Isabel a little while," Leocade said. "I'll bet you have never been in her house, have you?"

Eliza shook her head.

"Then stay. When I finish with Oscar and Joseph, I will be ready to visit with Regina," Leocade called as she pulled at the reins and turned Southern Belle toward the fields.

Eliza watched her ride away. "She's really something," she whispered to Oscar. "Has she always been that way?"

"Yep!" he answered. "Always."

Lady of the house

Joseph and Oscar walked shoulder to shoulder through the field to the horses. Eliza watched them for a moment, then opened the door to Joseph's house and called, "Isabel?" There was no answer. She walked into the front room. There were two chairs, a bed, and a chest on one end of the room. On the other end, there was a sewing machine like Idea's.

"Why, Miss Eliza," Isabel said as she walked into the room, "you're still here! I didn't know! I been out back trying to chase down that rooster again. He gives me all sorts of trouble!"

Eliza giggled. "I'm sorry, Isabel. I wanted to visit a little before I walked back to the house."

"Well, that's good. I would like that. Come back to the kitchen and I'll fix some coffee so we can talk."

The house was so small that with only a few steps Eliza was in the kitchen. She sat at the long dining table and watched as Isabel poured boiling water through the top of the coffeepot. The smell of fresh coffee filled the air, and Eliza realized that this was the only time she had ever been in the house of a worker. Isabel looked at her young mistress and smiled, "I'm glad to see you, Miss Eliza. It's not often the lady of the house has come to visit here."

Eliza knew what Isabel meant. "Mama D was once the lady of the house, wasn't she?"

"Yes," Isabel answered, "she was. Today, she rode up on her horse just like she used to. Did you know she was coming?"

"No," Eliza said. "Neither did Oscar."

"That's just like her, you know. Full of mischief and surprises."

Eliza looked around the kitchen. The walls were lined with shelves and pictures of people, all staring out from old wooden frames with sad eyes and expressionless mouths. One old man sat in a chair with a pipe in his mouth. Behind him was a closed door. There was a little boy too. He was all dressed up in a white shirt with a wide collar and short pants two sizes too big for his tiny frame. In his hand he held a book.

"Isabel," Eliza asked, "I would like to look at your sewing machine."

"Of course, Miss Eliza. Let's go to the front room and you can sit at it. Mr. Oscar told me you made a skirt once, an indigo skirt, and you wore it to the dance!"

The two women talked about children, and keeping a house clean, and making their families happy. Eliza sat at Isabel's sewing machine, and Isabel gave her a little piece of cloth to stitch. She liked the way the wheel felt in her hand, and the way her foot rested on the pedal.

"Did Joseph give you this?" she asked, running her hand across the top of the machine.

"Goodness, no!" Isabel laughed. "This was Miss Leocade's sewing machine. She got tired of it. Didn't have the time or the inclination anymore. She asked me to sew for the boys when they were little. Then they grew up and wanted only store bought clothes. So here I am with a nice sewing machine."

"Don't you sew for your two little girls?"

"Souri does that more than I do," Isabel answered. "You should see her work."

Eliza glanced out the window and realized Leocade and Oscar were probably waiting for her. "Isabel," she said. "I don't know if it's the proper thing for the lady of the house to visit the home of a worker, but I have had such a nice time here with you."

"That's all that matters, Miss Eliza," Isabel replied.

~ ~ ~ ~

"Where is your furniture, Oscar?" his mother asked, walking through the house.

Oscar studied his mother's face. "I don't see any point in filling rooms with pieces of furniture when there is no one to use them.

"Oh, I see. I guess I'm no one," she replied, holding her arms out to Regina. At first the baby didn't remember her, and then she smiled as her grandmother kissed her.

"Now mother, if you want to stay the night we can accommodate you." Oscar said.

"No, I have too much to do tomorrow," Leocade answered, "but I will stay a few minutes to play with Regina." She sat on the bench at the kitchen table, and setting Regina on the table, she held the baby's hands in hers.

"Pat a cake, pat a cake, baker man. Bake a cake as fast as you can. Roll it around. Roll it around. Mark it with a B, and put it in the oven for baby and me."

Regina laughed as her grandmother tickled her tummy. "Oh, I miss you," Leocade said, hugging her. For a second, Eliza thought Leocade might stay, but instead, she stood up, and handing Regina to Eliza, she walked toward the front room.

"If I leave now, I'll be home before sunset," she said. "That's the way I like it."

Eliza walked her to the door saying, "You must come back for the boucherie next month. Mama and Papa will be here."

"Well, I just might do that," she answered. Before Eliza and Oscar could give Leocade a proper good-by, she was gone.

"Oscar," Eliza asked, "did you tell your mother what you have named the plantation?'

"You mean, Eagle Crest?"

Souri giggled from the kitchen. "I like that name," she said. "I hope it never gets changed!"

"I like it too," Oscar replied. "But to answer your question, Cher, no, I don't think I ever told Mama."

"It doesn't matter to me if she knows or not," said Eliza. "I was just wondering if she would like the name."

"Miss Eliza," Souri said, "you got to know Mrs. D. On some particular days she might not like anything. So you have to be careful what day you tell her about the name." Souri smiled and rolled her big brown eyes. "Seems to me it's more important that you get that furniture made, Mr. Oscar."

CHAPTER SIX

THE MOON ROSE late that September night and hung close to the fields like a huge silver disc. Eliza knew the workers would pick tonight. "A harvest moon is the perfect time," Oscar said. "The heat of the day is gone, and the workers can finish an entire field in one night."

She could hear them now as they moved down the rows of cotton. Some hummed, some sang, and some hollered out the answer to the question asked in the song. The children were with them, little shadows along side the bigger ones. Oscar was there too, dressed in dark clothes so the workers couldn't find him.

"Hmmm."

"She married a carpenter man."

"Hmmm. Hmmm."

"How can she leave him?'

"Hmmm. Hmmm."

"She can marry me and live on the banks of the Mississippi."

"On the banks of the Mississippi."

"Hmmm. Hmmm."

Eliza stepped into the yard behind the kitchen. There was not a sound except for the singing. The dark skins blended into the night making the bolls of cotton dance in the darkness as though suspended in air before they disappeared into the white sacks. Suddenly, the singing stopped. Joseph was calling to the workers from the barn. The men let out yells and whoops, and the women cackled. The sacks fell to the ground, and the shadows moved toward the barn and the waiting jugs of whiskey. The children continued to pick the cotton, singing and humming as they moved along the rows.

"We got to pick this cotton."

"Hmmm. Hmmm. Before it gets too rotten."

~ ~ ~ ~

"Eliza woke with a start. "Souri! Souri!" Eliza called.

"Yes, Miss Eliza," Souri answered, looking through the door of the bedroom next to Eliza's. "I'm here with little Regina, right here, playing on the floor."

"Did the workers finish?"

"Yes, Ma'am," she answered. "I went to bed when that big moon went to bed. They had all just about finished by then."

Eliza looked at her husband's pillow. "Where is Oscar?" she asked.

"Mr. Oscar and Pappy have gone to town with the wagon full of cotton. He said he was in a hurry because it looked like rain."

Eliza shivered. The air was damp and somehow colder in the room. She looked out over the porch. The wind was picking up, making ripples in the top of the old oak tree. She and Isabel fixed lunch for the workers, and then they combed one of the sacks of cotton that Isabel had set aside.

"Someone surely did a good job picking out all the seeds," Eliza said.

"That's my sisters who did that," Souri answered. "They like to pull all that out of there and then tell me what kind of clothes to make for them."

The rain had just begun when Oscar and Joseph returned. With the summer heat gone, the rain came softly. There was just a

66

little thunder and a tiny bit of lightning, that's all. It was nothing like the show put on by the clouds during a summer heat storm when lightning streaks across the sky touching the earth with ropes of fire.

"Where's my girl?" Oscar asked, as he held out a doll with large blue eyes and a pink bonnet. Regina ran to her father and waited at his feet for him to pick her up. Wrapping her arms around his neck, she squealed with laughter as he kissed her on the cheek, and then she kissed the doll.

"What did my girl do today?" he asked.

"Mama," she answered, holding out both arms to Eliza.

"I got her a bag of candy too," Oscar said. "Can she have some now?"

Eliza looked at her husband, and taking the bag of candy from his hand, she dropped it into the pocket of her apron. "Maybe tomorrow," she said.

Sometime during the night the rain stopped, but morning came filled with clouds and the rumble of thunder in the distance. Eliza and Souri had just begun breakfast, when Joseph knocked at the front door, then opened it and ran in, gasping for breath. "Mr. Oscar," he called out, "Mr. Mouton needs our help. Everybody is sick over at his house, and the field is barely picked. More rain is on its way. All the cotton will be ruined unless we do something."

"Sit down, Joseph," Oscar said, pointing to a chair. "How do our workers feel about this?"

"I don't rightly know, Mr. Oscar. But I do know we need to do something tonight cause it's gonna be bad tomorrow. You can see it in the horses and the chickens. They is all over the place!"

"What do you propose?" Oscar asked.

"Load up the two wagons with every person that can work," Joseph answered. "Hitch up two horses to each wagon, and go to Mr. Mouton's before dark."

"What if there is no moon tonight?"

"Then we'll bring our lanterns, and make our own light."

"What is making the workers so sick, do you know?"

"No sir, I didn't ask. I figure we'll have to help no matter what it is because, well, they are supposed to help us with the boucherie."

Oscar knew Joseph was right, Eagle Crest would help not only because John and Mary Mouton had volunteered to bring a pig for the boucherie, but also because it was like money in the bank. When you helped someone, they helped you. By the time the wagons were all loaded with workers, big and little, it was late in the day.

"You all go on," Oscar told Joseph. "I'll saddle up and meet you after sunset."

As the wagons pulled away, the workers began to sing again, and Eliza saw the back of one of the wagons was lined with jugs of whiskey and every size of oil lanterns. A little sun had managed to break through the clouds, but now, with dusk, that was almost gone. The wind suddenly came up, blowing from the south.

Oscar looked at Eliza. "We may not make it. A south wind usually brings more rain."

By the time Oscar left, the almost full moon had risen, covering the low rain clouds with an eerie light. Regina was asleep, and Souri and Isabel had left on the wagons. Eliza stepped out on the front porch. The wind felt strange to her. First it ruffled her skirt like a breeze which blows across clothes hung out to dry. Then the air became very still. No animals moved about. The clouds were racing north, so low they seemed to touch the trees. The shutters on the house rattled ever so slightly. Eliza walked inside and bolted the door. Her hands shook as she lit another lantern.

She opened the chest Joseph had made, and moving some of her clothes, found the Bible her mother gave to her. As the wind and rain began to pound the doors and windows, she opened the Bible and discovered a ribbon which marked her mother's favorite passage from the Book of Psalms. "The Lord is my Shepherd: I shall not want. He makes me lie down in green pastures. He leads me to still waters where I may rest. He refreshes my soul. He takes me along paths that are straight for His name's sake. Though I walk in the valley of darkness, I will fear no evil because He is with me. His rod and His staff comfort me. He will prepare a table for me in the sight of my adversaries; He will anoint my head with oil; my cup overflows. Goodness and mercy shall follow me all the days of my life, and I will dwell in the house of the Lord forever."

Eliza heard what she guessed was a branch rolling across the porch. Something hit the back of the house. The wind began to whistle through the cracks in the doors. She extinguished the lanterns, and wrapping her sleeping baby tightly in a blanket, Eliza brought Regina into her own bed.

Although the storm continued, Eliza fell asleep, and when she awoke, the house was still. All she heard was the water dripping from the roof onto the wet leaves. She opened the front door and felt the cool air against her face. The old oak was a silhouette against a sky filled with stars, and all around she felt the night.

Oscar did not return until late the next day. The cotton had gotten wet, but a strong wind, and the morning sun dried the crop out enough for the workers to finish the harvest.

"Everyone is tired," he said. "And John and Mary are both sick."

"What is it?" Eliza asked.

"Yellow fever, I think," Oscar replied.

~ ~ ~ ~

The crops brought less money than ever before. Oscar took a total of two wagons of cotton to the gin and three wagons of sugar cane to the sugar mill. The corn was the worst of all. He had only a little to trade for corn meal and flour. However, there were lots of eggs which were always good to trade for tobacco and a new pair of shoes for Regina.

The Boucherie

The once lush fields were ragged now. Each day seemed shorter than the day before, and fall was slowly slipping into winter. Oscar decided that it was time for the boucherie when Eliza said if they waited much longer, Idea would not be able to make the trip.

On the day of the boucherie the sounds of wagons filled the early morning. The first to arrive were John and Mary Mouton with five of their workers and a pig named Martha. Their wagon was followed by two others stuffed with cousins, aunts, uncles, and grandparents.

"This is more fun than Christmas," hollered Souri as she watched John Mouton tie Martha to a tree. "I sure wish we could get started. I can already smell the gratons, and no one has started to cook yet!"

"Hush, Souri," John Mouton called out. "Martha will hear you!"

Leocade arrived on horseback, as usual, this time she was riding a white stallion named Mister. His mane was silver and it lay across his neck in thick sheets, making him look as though he was fashioned out of metal.

Alcide was holding the reins as the Landry buggy stopped near the front porch. Next to him was his father Charles, with Pierre, Edmond, Helen and Marie seated in the back.

"Where's Mama?" Eliza asked, tears filling her eyes.

Charles climbed out of the buggy, and hugging his daughter he said, "Dr. Gilbert put her to bed. He said the baby may come early, more like Christmas than January, and Christmas is only one month away. She sent you a present," he added, slipping a small box into her hand. "Wait until tonight to open it."

Eliza fingered the delicate white ribbon which held the box shut, and then slipped it into the pocket of her apron. "Come on, everyone," she said, "we've been waiting for you to get started."

"Oh, you shouldn't have," sang Pierre in a high voice. "We're only poor common folk, you know."

"The only thing poor about you is the size of your brain," Eliza answered.

Charles Landry helped Oscar and Joseph as they slaughtered the pig and hung her to bleed. There was a lot of hooping and yelling coming from the direction of the barn, and when Eliza looked out the kitchen window, she saw Pierre, Edmond, and Souri's brother Lucius dancing in a circle around a big iron pot in the center of the yard. Joseph was building a fire beneath the pot, and the flames climbed higher with each new piece of wood.

"There it is!" cried Souri. "That's what I've been waiting for!" She ran out the kitchen door and began to help her father. About

71

ten feet away, several of the workers shaved the hair off the pig's skin, sliced it into small strips, and tossed the strips into a large barrel. Oscar carried the barrel over to the pot, which was now filled with lard so hot that it shimmered. He dropped the pieces of raw skin into the pot. As he stirred, the lard bubbled up in great waves of foam, and the skins rose to the top. The children had already gathered around the cypress tables when Oscar scooped the gratons from the pot and spread them out to cool.

~ ~ ~ ~

"Ohhh, I don't think I can stand it," Souri said, pretending to faint and then grabbing a graton and stuffing it into her mouth. She quickly spit it out, blew on it, then stuffed it into her mouth once again. Rolling her eyes, she mopped her brow with the back of her hand. "Ahh, that was good!" she gasped.

Leocade had a small cotton sack which she quickly filled with hot gratons, and walking into the kitchen, she told Eliza, "I will be leaving soon, but I really enjoyed all this commotion." She walked into one of the front rooms, and then returned to the kitchen, saying, "Where is the new furniture Oscar promised you?"

Eliza laughed, "Don't be too hard on him, Mama D. He and Joseph spent a lot of time helping Mr. Mouton with his cotton crop. I think Joseph will have time now to make some furniture."

"You better remind him," Leocade replied, eating a graton. "I know what happens when those people drink too much of the juice, if you know what I mean."

At first, the sounds of music came softly from the direction of the old oak tree. Eliza heard the violin, and knew it was Lucius. Joseph had given him the violin for his birthday, a gift which made

Isabel proud since Lucius had always wanted to play an instrument. There were other sounds too: the shush shush of a washboard scraped with the back of a metal spoon, humming, and singing which Eliza identified as Souri and Pierre, and the clear ringing of a triangle which belonged to Abney, Mr. Mouton's stable boy. Soon the sounds became music, and onlookers called out words to the songs, clapping their hands and tapping their shoes as they danced to the rhythms. The instruments talked to each other, and the music filled the late afternoon air.

Leocade mounted her stallion, and rode away, traveling west, with the sack of gratons tied to the saddle horn. One by one the families left also, taking with them a share of Martha the pig. They sat in their wagons and hummed with the music as the sun began to slip behind the oaks which outlined the fields.

Eliza steeped the cooked pork in barrels filled with lard, and put all the gratons into large tins which were sealed and put on the kitchen shelf. Ham and sausage hung in the smokehouse. Isabel went home with Souri. Regina was asleep beside Oscar in the big bed. Eliza pulled out the present which lay hidden in the pocket of her apron. As she untied the tiny white bow the box opened, revealing a silver cross with a baby, kneeling in prayer in the center. Written on a note tied to the cross were these words, "Never underestimate the power of prayer."

CHAPTER SEVEN

WHEN OSCAR AND Eliza stood on the Pinhook Bridge and looked down the river, they could see the bonfires lighting the way for Papa Noel in his pirogue. The grand houses which sat on the banks of the river danced in the firelight, and the people appeared on the balconies like curious Christmas Eve ghosts. Papa Noel was expected around midnight. It was rumored he never traveled on land in this part of the country because of the alligators, although everyone knows the gators could have been used to pull a buggy if they had been well fed.

Regina looked steadily at the reflections of the bonfires. "Papa Noel, Mama. Papa Noel," she said.

"He's coming," Eliza answered. "But you have to be asleep if you want some toys."

There were other people watching the bonfires from the bridge. Groups singing carols walked along Pinhook Road stopping at the houses and businesses. There were buggies and surreys decorated with garland and piled high with blankets and picnic baskets. As the darkness deepened, and the buggies and surreys left, the carolers disappeared. By the time Eliza and Oscar returned to Eagle Crest, Regina had fallen asleep in her mother's arms. As Eliza lay in bed, she thought about Idea and Christmas Day, and wondered if the baby would be born early as the doctor had said.

Surely I would have been told if the baby had arrived early, she thought. Eliza did find it strange though that Pierre had not come to visit. He usually bothered them for something at least once a week. He's probably helping Papa, she decided. She fell into a fitful sleep, and awakened with a start around midnight. Her heart was racing, and she was trembling. Then it all passed, and when she fell asleep again, it was deep and peaceful, and she was awakened in the morning by Regina laughing with Oscar.

"Merry Christmas, Cher," Oscar said, poking his sleepy wife in the arm.

"Papa Noel?" Regina asked.

"Yes!" Oscar said. "Let's go find out what he brought!"

Oscar opened the front door. "Come see, my little one," he said, motioning to Regina. She squealed when she found the toys piled high on the front porch. "That is the sweetest sound there is," Eliza said as she watched Regina open her presents.

Eliza and Oscar sang Christmas songs to Regina as they rode to Côte Gelée to spend the rest of Christmas with Idea and Charles. Eliza had decorated the surrey with a garland of red jingle bells and there was not one person along the way who did not stop and wave.

"Merry Christmas," the strangers called out. "Merry Christmas to you too," Oscar, Eliza, and Regina called in return.

"Did you see Papa Noel?" one man asked.

"No," Oscar called back. "Did you?"

"No, he was too quick for me," the man replied. "But I know he was here because he slid his pirogue up onto the bank of the river just behind my house. No doubt he was resting a little before returning to the North Pole."

Regina's eyes were wide, and she looked at Eliza with her lip trembling. "Don't worry," Eliza said. "He'll return next Christmas if you are good."

~ ~ ~ ~

The lush green trees which lined the road during the summer had disappeared, leaving behind a maze of twisted branches to rake the clear, cold morning sky. Eliza wrapped another blanket around Regina, and she watched the baby's breath form little clouds of fog. They were almost there.

No one came to meet the surrey as it pulled up to the house. There were no voices laughing and singing. Suddenly Oscar began to laugh, gesturing toward the front porch and the woman who was standing there.

"Who is that?" Eliza asked.

"Don't you recognize NaNoot a Les Yeux Vert," Oscar answered.

"When Marie was born," Eliza said, "she was there, I remember! Oh, Oscar, take Regina, I have to go inside." With that, she jumped from the surrey and ran into the house.

NaNoot shook her head and laughed. "It's been awhile since I saw Miss Eliza," she said. "She sure is a pretty thing."

Oscar followed Eliza into the house. "NaNoot," he said, "this is my daughter Regina. Do you remember her?"

"Indeed I do, Mr. Oscar. And look at yourself, all grown up and handsome, too. That baby looks like you, can't deny that, you know."

The front room was empty. Oscar walked through the door which led to the back bedroom and found Eliza sitting on the bed, holding little Julie. The new born baby's tiny hands rested on the blanket, making her look all the more like a tiny china doll. Idea lay with her eyes closed and her hand resting in the hand of her husband asleep next to her.

"Mama, how will you be able to do everything you need to do for yourself and for Julie?" Eliza asked.

Idea opened her eyes and looked at her oldest daughter. "There is no other purpose to my life than to do for my children and your father. Julie is a gift from God to an old lady like me. He sent her because she has a message from Emelie, I'm certain of that, and I am also certain my daughters will help me care for her."

NaNoot walked up, and putting her hand on Eliza's shoulder, she said, "Don't worry. Your mother is a strong lady, and she will be all right. What you see in her face is fatigue, that's all. Julie was born not more than ten hours ago at midnight." She took Julie from Eliza's arms, gave her to Idea and then said, "Come, we have Christmas to celebrate, and they need to sleep."

"Your mother had a difficult time, Miss Eliza," NaNoot said as they walked to the kitchen. "Little Julie took her own sweet time, and I was afraid for a little while that she might be backing into this world, but the Lord was with us, and she got herself born head first."

"Is Mama going to be all right now?" Eliza asked, her eyes filling with tears.

"Oh, my yes!" NaNoot answered. "Better than ever, in fact. And all of your brothers and sisters, they helped as much as they could, but it took its toll on them too, you know."

"What about Papa?"

NaNoot put her finger across her lips and said, "Shhhh, don't tell your mama, but he slept through the whole thing."

~ ~ ~ ~

After all the presents had been opened, Eliza thought about a Christmas morning long ago. Papa had cut down a tree, and Mama had decorated it and Eliza and Alcide were the only children who were allowed to help because they were the oldest. Pierre was there, and so was Edmond. Emelie was there too, playing with Helen and Marie. As Eliza shut her eyes, she saw her room as it was then. She saw Emelie, singing and laughing in front of a mirror which hung over the dresser. So vivid was the scene that Eliza walked into her old room, and standing in front of the mirror, she held her breath, half expecting to see Emelie. Instead, the bedroom door opened and she saw Souri's brother Lucius staring at her.

"What are you doing here?" Eliza gasped.

Lucius took a deep breath and said, "This morning Pierre was asleep, Alcide was asleep, Edmond was asleep, Helen was asleep, and Marie was asleep. The only one who wasn't asleep was the baby. Aunt NaNoot said, well Lucius, it's up to you and me to get Christmas ready for this family. So here I am."

"Why aren't you with Souri and your parents?" Eliza asked.

"Duty calls," Lucius sniffed.

"No, it doesn't," Pierre called out from the dining room. "You just like the food over here better!"

Ignoring Pierre, Lucius continued. "Aunt NaNoot asked me to ask y'all if y'all are finished with the presents. She said we best eat now because the mama and her new baby will probably need her before too long."

Thanks be to God that NaNoot came early," gasped Helen. "We were scared to death!"

"That's right," said Marie. "I thought sure Mama was going to die!"

NaNoot looked at both girls. "Now really," she said, "it wasn't that bad. That's what it's like when someone is having a baby."

"We thought Julie was too little, and wouldn't live past one hour!" cried Marie. "Oh Eliza, it was terrible."

Eliza looked sternly at both her sisters. "It seems to me you forgot the most important part of a birth."

"What is that," both girls asked together.

"The presence of God," Eliza replied. "Had you remembered Him you would not have been frightened."

"I know why we forgot," Helen said. "Mama was too busy having Julie to remind us."

Eliza shook her head. "That's no excuse. You are both too old to need Mama to remind you that God is always with you. You must trust in God and in His goodness, especially in the birth of a child because that child is a gift from Him."

~ ~ ~ ~

"We should leave soon, Cher," Oscar called from the hallway. "As soon as the sun goes down it will get colder."

Eliza had already said good-bye to her parents and little Julie, and she was helping NaNoot bring the presents and some of the food to the surrey. Regina was asleep in Pierre's arms.

"Look, Eliza, she likes me," he said.

"How can you tell?" Eliza answered. "She's asleep."

The sun was just above the horizon, and long shadows stretched ahead of Eliza and Oscar as they began the journey home to Eagle Crest. Eliza was not aware of the sounds made by the horse pulling the surrey along the dirt roads. Nor did she hear the crickets singing softly in the ditches. Her thoughts were back in Côte Gelée, back in the house filled with babies many years ago. She heard the laughter and the sweet good-byes that came all too soon. She knew she had changed, and as surely as the shadows chase the sunset she would change more.

CHAPTER EIGHT

WHEN OSCAR WAS twenty-four years old, Eliza celebrated her eighteenth birthday. She pretended to enjoy her dinner, but, in reality she felt sick. When Easter Sunday arrived just one week later she did not attend mass with Oscar and Regina.

"But where is Eliza?" Charles Landry asked as he walked to meet Oscar at the Chapel of St. John.

"She is not feeling well again," Oscar said, and looking at Idea he winked. "I believe this may take at least nine months to pass."

"Ah ha," Charles laughed. "So it was not something she ate after all!"

"I knew it!" Idea said. "Does she suspect she is pregnant?"

Oscar shrugged his shoulders. "I don't know. We haven't talked much about this. She thinks it might be caused by the fasting for Easter, but she has fasted for Easter before, and it never made her feel like this."

April turned into May, and then into June and summer. The nausea left Eliza, but now she was beginning to show fullness around her waist. There was no denying what would happen in six months. Oscar was elated, and often said he would be content to spend the rest of his life cultivating his crops and tending to his plantation with his sons. Eliza on the other hand spent many hours in front of the sewing machine which Oscar had given to her as a birthday present.

~ ~ ~ ~

"How do you know she wants a sewing machine?" Oscar asked Souri.

"Because Momma told me," Souri replied. "Miss Eliza went over to her house and saw her sewing machine and even sat and sewed on a little piece of cloth. That sewing machine used to belong to your mama and you need to ask her where she got it."

When Oscar told his mother that he intended to buy Eliza a sewing machine, she looked at him for a few minutes and then said, "Are you certain you want to buy this now? Why not buy her something pretty for the house, a new blanket for your bed perhaps, or maybe a warm sweater to wear when she takes the baby outside in the winter?"

"Well, I am thinking her parents would not give her a sewing machine, but they might give her something to wear," Oscar replied. "Where should I go to buy a sewing machine?"

"Well," Leocade took a deep breath, "I know that your father bought mine at Jim Higginbotham's shop near the Pinhook Bridge. It was a brand new thing, you know, and not too many people sold them. Jim might still be selling them; I don't know. I do know he quit selling spinning wheels because most people buy all the thread and fabric they need instead of making it. Your father gave me the sewing machine just before he died. I never really had a chance to use it because, after he died I was too busy managing his affairs and my land, and raising you and your brothers. I had no time to sew outfits for five little boys. Isabel was always a loyal servant, and I knew Souri would learn to sew if there was a sewing machine in the house."

Oscar thought often about the conversation with his mother that day. He realized the death of his father placed a burden on Leocade that changed her life forever. He always felt she was the strong one, but she was still a woman and must have wanted nice things, like a new blanket or a soft sweater. She chose instead a new bridle for her horse.

In only a short time, Oscar was envied as a successful plantation owner. He had over thirty loyal workers, at least five fields of sugar cane and cotton, and a smaller one of corn. His pond was filled with crawfish, bream, and sac-a-lait. The orchards produced an abundance of oranges, pears, peaches and pecans. There were gardens with potatoes, tomatoes, beans and peanuts. He had bottles of wine made from the grapes which grew along the fence next to the house. His cattle and horses were some of the finest, and he always had enough eggs to swap for new shoes and clothes for Eliza and Regina.

When it came time for the harvest, Oscar worked in the fields night and day. This year's crop was much better. There had been enough rain and enough sun. The cotton bolls were full, and white as snow. The sugar cane grew taller than it had ever grown, and with his mother's sugar press, he had pure cane syrup each morning to pour over Eliza's biscuits.

"You work so hard," Eliza told him. "Take a little rest now. Let me fix your pipe for you, and sit and talk to me."

"How do you feel, Cher?" he asked his young wife. "You look tired, and I can see that you are uncomfortable."

Eliza yawned. "I am tired. The baby seems to move constantly. And I wonder if he is all right."

"Do you think it will be a boy?"

"Each time I think of the baby, I think of a boy," she replied. "By the way," she continued, "your mother should be visiting us soon. Remember, she said she wanted to discuss something with us when I was close to having the baby."

"What do you think she wants to talk about?" Oscar asked.

Eliza handed her husband his pipe. "I haven't the slightest idea," she said, "but I am sure it is important."

The two of them sat and looked at the October sky filled with stars. A few lanterns were still burning in the little houses which sat in a row on the other side of the field. Souri's day was done, and she walked towards those lights, a silhouette against the dark horizon, her white shawl tracing her departure.

"I have something to ask you," Eliza said.

Oscar looked at his wife and reached out his hand. "When I was little," Eliza began, "I was never allowed to spend much time with the servants. They were there to work and do as Mama said. I never saw them eat, and I never knew if they ever ate or where they lived. I remember them getting sick, but they had their own doctors. Papa did pay for their care. I know because he always handed them money in an envelope to pay the doctor. I don't know if Mama ever gave them anything. How is it that you are different towards the workers here on the plantation? Weren't you and I taught the same?"

Oscar shook his head. "No. My mother knew she could not manage all the land by herself. My brothers and I learned to respect all the workers, and if they were not well-fed or got sick, why, then it was up to us to feed them properly and take care of them. The workers, in turn, were allowed to grow gardens to feed their families and gather moss to sell as stuffing for beds of white people. As a little boy, I played with the children of the workers,

84

and as a young man I learned to ride horses from Mama's stable boy."

Eliza took a deep breath. "The day you asked for my hand in marriage, Mama spoke to me about freed slaves and colored people. She told me I was not like them and I must hold myself apart from them. After seeing Eagle Crest and the people who work here, I do not know if I can do that."

"That will come, Cher," Oscar replied. "Give this time. You were taught to be afraid. Now you will have to learn to trust."

~ ~ ~ ~

Leocade paid a visit to Eliza and Oscar on a crystal clear November morning. She appeared out of the west riding Mister right up to the kitchen door, throwing Souri into such a tizzy that she dropped the basket of eggs she had gathered for breakfast.

"I declare Mrs. D, you sure do know how to scare a body!" Souri gasped. "You must be here to see Mr. Oscar, cause I know it's not me."

Leocade held her skirt up as she walked through the broken eggs. "Lord child, what a mess! Where is that son of mine?"

"I guess maybe in the kitchen, waiting for some breakfast," Souri answered. "If you going that way, tell Mr. Oscar and Miss Eliza I'm going to be here awhile."

"Oscar," Leocade called, "where are you?"

"Mama? Is that you?"

"Are all your mornings like this one?" Leocade asked as she walked into the kitchen and sat down at the table.

Oscar grinned. "No, only the ones with you in them!"

"I thought I might join you for breakfast," she said, "but since Souri has dropped all the eggs, I guess I will have to make other plans."

Oscar laughed. "Oh, so that is what is holding everything up. There are more eggs where those came from. Watch how quickly I can fix breakfast."

After the eggs and grits had been devoured, and the coffee pot was empty, Oscar and his mother rode through the fields. When they returned at mid-morning, Leocade motioned for Oscar and Eliza to follow her into the front room.

"I want to talk to you about Regina," she said. "I think you should decide now what you will tell Regina about her mother, and what you will tell your children about Regina."

"What do you mean?" Eliza asked. "We have never discussed this, probably because it doesn't seem to be a problem. Regina will always be our first born."

"Remember, if you do not tell Regina the truth, she will never know who her real mother was, and there is a danger that someone in the Boudreau family might tell her when she is older. I know those people because I am a Boudreau."

Eliza looked at Oscar. "Do you think this is possible?"

"Perhaps," he replied. "It might be best if we told her when she is old enough."

"And what about the other children?" Leocade continued. "What will you tell them?"

Oscar thought for a moment. "I will tell the children that Regina is their sister," he said.

~ ~ ~ ~

The time eventually came for Regina to move from her parents' room to "her room," as Eliza called the smaller room behind Eliza and Oscar's own bedroom. Joseph made a child's bed out of the smooth, light brown wood of a sweet gum tree, and he carved Regina's name across the headboard. He asked his son Jefferson to make a matching chest of drawers and add a mirror "because all ladies like mirrors."

Jefferson knew a lot about furniture. He once worked for Mr. Higginbotham who not only sold sewing machines, but he also made hickory chairs with rawhide seats. Jefferson had a seven year old boy named William. When the furniture was finished, William helped his father and grandfather bring it all to Oscar's house and set it on the front porch.

"Miss Eliza," Joseph called, "where do you want us to put Regina's new furniture?" Eliza led them to Regina's room, and as Joseph and Jefferson assembled the bed, Eliza looked at William and said, "Hello, what's your name?" William's eyes grew wide. "Hello," she said again. "What's your name?"

"He don't talk much, Miss Eliza," Joseph said. "But he does understand what you say."

Eliza could feel William watching as she spread sheets and a blanket on Regina's new bed. When she walked up to him, he ran behind his father. "Where is that boy!" she called out, looking inside the new chest of drawers and behind the door. "I know he is here somewhere, and if he comes out I will give him a surprise!"

William watched Eliza from his hiding place on the other side of the bed.

"William? William, where are you?" she called again.

"It's no use Miss Eliza," Joseph said. "That boy just won't get a surprise, that's all. He must want to hide like a girl." Even that insult didn't bring William out of his refuge. "We are going home now," Joseph said. "If you want a little boy, you can have him." With those words, Joseph and Jefferson left the house and began to walk across the pasture.

Eliza sighed. "Oh well, I think I will go into the kitchen. There is no little boy here anymore." After waiting awhile in the kitchen, she went back into Regina's room. William was now gone. Looking out the front door, Eliza saw him running across the pasture toward his grandpa's house.

~ ~ ~ ~

Every Monday was Wash Day. Isabel was usually in charge, but this day she was ill. "Pappy," Souri said to Joseph, "make certain you put enough big pieces of wood under that pot. You know how Miss Eliza likes the wash water to stay hot hot!"

"Yes Ma'am!" Joseph replied, clearing his throat. "You can start filling the pot with water now."

Soon the water began to simmer. Souri disappeared into the house and returned with her apron full of soap chips, which she dropped into the hot water. "Can you smell that?" she asked. "I don't know if I like the way the soap smells when it's in a pot of boiling water! But don't worry now, that smell won't keep me from washing."

Souri tossed the clothes into the pot and stirred with a boat paddle, turning her head to the side to avoid the clouds of steam. "Oh Lord," she gasped. "I don't want to do this too often!"

When Eliza learned that Isabel was ill, and Jefferson was going to take her to a traiteur, she asked Souri if she had ever been to a traiteur. "Oh yes, Miss Eliza," Souri answered. "One time I had the croup, so Momma took me to this lady traiteur who lived on the edge of a swamp. It was in the middle of winter. She lit some candles, and right away she said some prayers, asking help from God and from the Blessed Mother of Jesus, too. She rubbed my throat with wax, and sprinkled my head with water. The water had been blessed and it was very powerful for curing most anything. Then she put both her hands on my shoulders, but she was standing behind me, and she pressed real hard, all the while yelling out dead people's names and talking funny. The whole thing ended when she made the sign of the cross a bunch of times, and then she fell to the floor, like she was dead. I think it had something to do with getting the healing started inside of me."

"Were you cured, Souri?"

"Not right then. I had to wait until the full moon for the curing to work. But it did, and I felt real good after that!"

Eliza nodded her head. "I've heard the moon has an effect on people," she said. "This is all very strange. Will Isabel go during a full moon?"

"Yes Ma'am! She says she needs the moon to get as much curing as she can. That moon does do wonders. Why, everyone knows a full moon is good for having babies and getting married."

Eliza rubbed her abdomen. "When is the next full moon, Souri?"

Souri looked at Eliza and gasped, "Oh! I didn't realize how close you are to having this baby! Maybe I should tell Pappy to fetch Aunt NaNoot so she will be here in plenty of time."

Three days later Joseph brought his sister to Eagle Crest. NaNoot walked up to Eliza and hugged her gently. "How are you feeling, Miss Eliza?" she asked.

"I guess I feel all right," Eliza answered. "But I am very tired."

"Let's go inside and I will show you how to rest. You have been doing too much and that is not good." NaNoot turned back the covers on the bed and plumped the pillows. "Now take those shoes off, lie down and go to sleep."

Eliza shut her eyes. Even the movements of the baby stopped, and Eagle Crest seemed to fall asleep also. She dreamed of the tiny life she held inside of her. She saw the baby's face, but did not know whether it was a boy or a girl. She heard the baby laugh, and in her mind it sounded like Regina's laugh on Christmas morning. Then, in her dreams, she heard the sound of water and felt a sharp pain across her abdomen. Eliza awoke with a start. She looked around the room. Her heart was pounding in her ears and then suddenly, the dream and the pain were gone.

The last days of her pregnancy raced by. Each afternoon NaNoot placed her hand on Eliza's abdomen and pressing hard, she said she could feel one of the baby's feet, or sometimes, the head. Eliza often placed her hand over NaNoot's and followed the movement of NaNoot's strong fingers across her abdomen.

Oscar and Eliza spent Christmas morning opening presents with Regina while Souri and Isabel tried to make Eagle Crest festive by softly singing carols as they prepared a holiday meal. During the afternoon, Pierre surprised his sleeping sister with a buggy full of presents from Charles and Idea. Eliza was awakened by his voice and covered her head with a pillow just as Pierre walked into the house.

"Eliza!" he whispered. "Why are you asleep in the middle of the day?"

"Because," she whispered from under the pillow, "I'm about to have a baby, you idiot."

"I have some presents for you," he whispered again. "What do you want me to do with them?"

Eliza pulled the pillow away and looked at her brother. "Where are they?" she asked.

"In the buggy. I'll get them." Pierre said. He returned with an armload of presents and put them at the foot of Eliza's bed.

Eliza awoke early the next morning. She pulled the covers away and stood up next to the bed. She felt wonderful, as though she had awakened from a long sleep. Pulling a shawl around her shoulders, she went into the kitchen. She was hungry.

NaNoot heard Eliza get out of bed and asked, "What are you doing awake?"

"I want to fix breakfast," Eliza answered.

NaNoot held Eliza's hand as she walked her to the table. "Sit down, child. I'll fix breakfast." She was making coffee when she heard Eliza cry out with the first pain. "Come, Miss Eliza," NaNoot said, "come back to bed. It is time."

Edward's IOU

After the birth of Edward, days quickly became months. Regina learned to sing to her little brother and he often fell asleep with his sister by his side. Oscar allowed each one of the workers to see Edward through the open bedroom window. The baby stared at each face as it appeared, and sometimes cried when someone yelled out "Hallelujah!" or "Praise the Lord!" After the workers had gone, Joseph asked if his grandson, William, could see Edward. Eliza was holding Edward as William walked into the room, carrying the biggest sunflower Eliza had ever seen. The stalk was as tall as William, and the blossom as big as his face. Edward's eyes widened, and a smile crossed his tiny lips and spread across his face like sunshine. He laughed, and Eliza laughed also as William handed the sunflower to her and ran back to hide behind his grandfather.

In six short years NaNoot returned four more times. She delivered the first girl, Cady, and then Gabriel, and Ida, and Jules. With five babies in the house, Regina became the perfect baby sitter, and she and Oscar spent many nights singing lullabies together. Souri and Isabel took over the house, cooking for the workers and managing the wash days. During those first years as a mother Eliza found herself steeped in rocking babies to sleep and midnight feedings. She had little time to sew on her new machine, but when she did, she made tiny overalls and little dresses with lace around the collars.

When Edward was seven years old, he decided to become a farmer, just like his father. Oscar was not aware that his first son even knew how to open the barn door, so when he discovered some of the farm implements missing he immediately accused Joseph of being careless.

"No sir, Mister Oscar, I didn't lose any tools," Joseph insisted. "You know how careful I am, sir!"

"Well, then, who do you suppose could have taken the tools?" Oscar asked.

"I don't rightly know, sir. But Miss Eliza might."

When Oscar asked Eliza where his tools were, she looked at him with surprise and said, "Where is Edward? I thought he was with you!"

"He can't open the barn door, can he?" Oscar asked.

"Yes, he can, Papa!" Regina sang out. "He did it the other day, even after I told him not to."

It took Oscar just a few minutes to locate Edward behind the barn. "Son, what are you doing with my new tools?" he asked.

"Planting a garden, just like you, Papa!" Edward answered. "Look how much dirt I have dug up already."

Oscar took the shovel from Edward's hands and began to turn over the large clumps of top soil, exposing the dark rich dirt underneath. "You must break the soil up, Edward, so that the seeds you plant will grow quickly." Oscar handed his son the rake, and standing behind him, he placed his large hands over Edward's small ones. The two of them moved the rake back and forth across the dry soil.

Edward looked at his father and grinned. "But Papa," he said, "you are doing all the work and I am the farmer. Will I have to pay you?"

"Do you have any money?" Oscar asked.

"No," Edward replied.

"Then I will write an IOU for you, and then you must sign it." Oscar said.

The two of them walked to the kitchen where Oscar found a pencil and a small scrap of paper. He wrote the words, "I owe my papa money for farm work," and handed the scrap of paper to Edward and said, "Sign your name on the bottom of this paper."

"But I can't sign my name. I don't know how. I have to finish first grade for that."

"Very well then, make the letter 'E' for Edward, and then the letter 'D' for Daigle. Can you do that?"

"Yes, I can!" Edward said, smiling.

The IOU was signed and stuck to the wall by the kitchen door. "I will remind you of this from time to time," Oscar said. "I expect payment, eventually."

"Yes, sir," Edward whispered.

The first year, Edward's garden was not very big, but there was room for a row of sunflowers across the back fence. Joseph's grandson William was a frequent visitor to the garden and he often fingered the sunflowers, obviously remembering the time he had given a sunflower to Edward when he was only a baby.

Anna was born when Edward was eight years old. The morning after Anna's birth, Edward realized that the girls now outnumbered the boys.

"Mama," he asked, "why are there more girls than boys? Do you think this is fair?"

Eliza laughed, "I do not decide whether to have a boy or a girl. God sends me what He wishes to send me!"

"Why was she born at midnight?" Edward asked.

"I don't decide the time either," Eliza replied.

Edward dug his hands in his pockets. "Seems sneaky to me."

When Regina became a boarder at the all-girls school called The Convent, Edward assumed his new duties as the baby sitter. He really didn't mind that there was one less girl to contend with, and best of all, he got to drive the buggy with Oscar. His job as baby sitter was short lived, however. He began school later that same year, and soon discovered that the school was named The Convent because it was run by a group of nuns. "More girls," he mumbled as he walked home from school the first day.

Regina's secret

Regina thrived as a boarder. The Convent was considered a finishing school for older girls, and those who attended learned how to cook and sew. Regina soon demonstrated a talent for making hats and her friends teased her, saying that she might become a famous milliner one day.

Oscar and Eliza visited Regina often and liked trips to The Convent to visit Regina because they were both reminded of their own education.

"Cher," Oscar asked, "When I was little I never went to school, did you?"

"I didn't go to school either," Eliza replied. "I had a tutor for everything."

"I had a tutor also," Oscar said. "I remember him well. He came to our house twice a week and we learned a lot about taking care of a plantation and running it like a business. I suppose that was because we were boys."

Oscar turned the horse through the gates of the school and brought the surrey to a stop at the steps of the main building. Normally Regina would have been waiting for them, but instead they were greeted by the school principal, a tall thin nun dressed in a long brown habit with a fluted cap and a black veil.

"I am glad you are here," she said. "Something has happened, and Regina is not feeling well."

"What is wrong?" Eliza asked. "Where is she?"

The nun led Oscar and Eliza to a tiny parlor which was adjacent to the office area. "Wait here," she said. "I'll go and get Regina."

"She can't be too sick if she can walk out to meet us," Oscar said. "What could be the problem?"

When Regina walked into the parlor, Eliza felt a strange feeling in the pit of her stomach. "What is it, Regina?" Eliza asked, hugging her tightly. Receiving no answer, she held Regina's face between her hands and repeated, "What is it?"

"Why didn't you tell me about my mother," Regina replied, her voice sharp with pain.

A heavy silence filled the parlor. Oscar sat down in one of the chairs. He could hear the faint chirping of birds in the fig trees which grew in a courtyard.

"We thought it would be best to wait and tell you when you were old enough to understand," Eliza said.

"And when would I be old enough?" Regina asked, her eyes filling with tears.

Oscar rubbed his forehead. "Who told you?"

"Mary Boudreau," Regina replied. "She said she was a cousin and knew all along that my mother died giving birth to me."

"I'm sorry you had to find out this way," he said. "I hoped it would be different. If you want to blame someone, blame me."

Regina walked to her father. "And what good would that do? How could you keep this from me for so long? I thought I belonged with you and now I don't know where I belong. I have so many questions now."

"What are they?" Oscar asked.

"Did she love me, even though she never saw me?"

"I'll answer that," Eliza said. "All mothers love their unborn children more than they love themselves. They would all give their own lives so that their babies might live. You have never seen God, but you still love Him, don't you?"

"Papa," Regina sobbed, "did she suffer?"

Oscar looked toward the two women who stood side by side, and with tears streaming down his face, he said, "No, Regina, she did not suffer. She slipped away peacefully, as though she had fallen asleep."

"Do you have a picture of her, Papa? Do I look like her?"

"No," Oscar replied, shaking his head. "Unfortunately, you look like me."

"What will we tell the others?" Regina asked.

Oscar looked at his daughter. "Do you want us to tell them? What do you want us to say?"

Regina was silent for a while. How strange life is, she thought. Something which happened to me so long ago is reaching out to me now, like the ripples a stone makes when tossed into the water.

"I don't want my brothers and sisters to know right now," she said, "because I think I am a Daigle, just as much as any one in this family. But I do think someone should be trusted with the secret, to tell after I am dead, or whenever the time seems right."

"Do you want me to choose?" Oscar asked.

"No, I want Mama to decide which one will keep the secret," Regina replied.

Oscar and Eliza rode home in silence. Although Eliza accepted Regina's decision, the choice of which child would keep the secret raced through her mind. She watched her husband's profile against the houses and trees.

"What are you thinking, Cher?" Oscar asked.

Eliza sighed. "I don't know who I should ask to keep the secret."

"You don't have to decide now," he replied. "Give this time. God may choose someone for you."

CHAPTER NINE

BY THE TIME Lucille was born, Lafayette had grown. The countryside was still country, there was just less of it. The Jefferson Theater was built on the street which ran through the heart of town and there was a bank also, and a drug store where a person could buy almost anything. The new high school was called "modern" because it had indoor water pipes and electricity, and a telephone so someone could call for a ride if Little Willie's horse-drawn bus couldn't wait. There were no gas stations yet, and no hospitals. People still needed wells and cisterns and Monday Wash Days. Board sidewalks lined the city streets, which were still narrow and dusty, and turned to mud when it rained.

One Sunday each month Charles and Idea Landry rode in their surrey to Eagle Crest to visit Eliza and Oscar. They packed their surrey with an entire lunch, complete with wine and fresh milk, and a large watermelon for dessert. Leaving Côte Gelée at ten in the morning, they arrived at Eagle Crest a little before noon. Pierre was always with them, and sometimes they also brought Julie.

Eliza and Oscar spread blankets under the old oak, and Souri brought plates and glasses from the kitchen in a big wash tub. Idea's picnic lunch was always fried chicken, biscuits with honey, and roasted corn on the cob. After everyone had finished, Charles placed the large watermelon in the washtub and prepared to cut it.

"Be careful," Pierre said. "Last time you cut a watermelon that big I got seeds in my ears when I bit into a slice."

Charles laughed. "Well, son, don't take such a big bite and you won't have to clean your ears." He held the knife firmly in his hand

and using all of his strength he split the watermelon open. Suddenly Charles dropped the knife, grabbed his chest and coughing, he fell to his knees.

"Charles!" Idea screamed. "Charles! What is wrong?"

As Charles fell forward, Oscar rushed to catch him, bracing his fall with his own body. "Take it easy," he whispered. "Just lie still until we can get some help."

Eliza loosened her father's shirt and belt as Idea tried to cradle his head in her lap. Souri picked up Julie who had begun to cry, and held her tightly.

"It's his heart, Miss Eliza," Souri said. "We best get him to a doctor."

"But look at him," Eliza said, "he is in such pain. Isn't there something to take that away?"

Souri motioned to Pierre. "Go to Momma's house, straight across the field. Tell her what's happened. She'll give you some purple leaves for Mr. Charles. Hurry!"

Isabel walked onto the porch just as Pierre reached the house. "What is it child?" she asked.

"It's my father," Pierre cried out. "He's hurting. He's grabbing at his chest and lying in the grass coughing."

Isabel went into the kitchen. On a shelf next to the stove was a small bottle filled with dark purple leaves. She placed two leaves in a small square of cloth and folded the ends together. "Put this in your pocket, Mr. Pierre, and take it to your father. Tell Miss Idea to put a piece of a leaf in your daddy's mouth and tell him to chew it. Hold his head up a little so he doesn't choke."

Although Charles was barely conscious by the time Pierre returned, Idea tried placing a piece of a leaf between his lips.

100

"Please, darling," Idea whispered, "try to chew this." His mouth moved slightly, and then he stopped breathing.

Eliza stared at her father. "Mama," she whispered, "wake him up so he can chew the leaf."

Idea caressed her husband's head. "Oh, my darling, I am not ready to let you go. There is so much I want to do with you. Please stay a little longer." The light in his face gradually slipped away and Eliza and Pierre watched as their father died.

After the funeral Eliza could not remember the moments before her father's death. Instead, she saw herself with him as he took her to the dance. She wore the shoes he had bought for her, the ones she always hung from the ceiling of her room. She laughed when she thought about her wedding day, when he laid a broomstick across the front door, and how could she forget his words to the wedding guests, "The daughter is now a woman. The son is now a man. And all the wishes in the world cannot erase the hand of time." Now Eliza realized she would not see her father again for a very long time.

~ ~ ~ ~

When the school year started that fall the nuns welcomed four Daigle children, Regina, Edward, Cady and Gabriel. Ida was only five, and although she thought she should be allowed to go to school, the nuns insisted she had to be seven years old. Jules and Anna became steadfast friends because they stayed with Eliza while the older ones climbed into the surrey for the daily ride to The Convent. When Edward was twelve he was allowed to take everyone to school and was told he could bring everyone home at the end of the day. The fact that it had rained during the night didn't bother Edward. He had driven the surrey with Oscar many times after a rain. I can handle a little mud, he thought. Edward also knew that the horse was afraid of automobiles, but he decided he probably wouldn't see one of those that morning. As he turned the surrey toward Lafayette his sisters Cady and Ida were sitting behind him. Gabriel was sitting next to him.

"So you think you are really something, right?" Gabriel asked. "How come no one lets me take the surrey?"

"Because you're too young, that's why!" Edward shot back.

Gabriel pretended to choke with laughter. "I suppose you are the only one here who is old enough to do anything!"

Edward stared ahead at the muddy road. The horse's hooves were already throwing up little clods of dirt which stuck to the sides of the surrey. He turned around to look at his sisters. They were all dressed in white, with ribbons in their hair. Suddenly he realized the horse was pulling to the side, and acting as though he was ready to bolt. Before Edward could tighten his grip on the reins, a black automobile rounded the corner. Mud flew in all directions as the horse ran as fast as the wind, heading straight for the school. He sailed through the open gates with everyone holding on to the top and sides of the surrey. Failing to make the final curve, the horse and surrey overturned in the grass along the side of the road, just a few feet from the entrance to the school. Covered with mud, the children crawled out from beneath the surrey and looked at each other. Edward and Gabriel burst into laughter as they saw their sisters' soggy curls and hair ribbons. Their dresses had completely changed color, and their shoes were filled with brown ooze.

"Aw, come on, don't cry now!" Edward said in response to the wails which filled the air. "Let's go to the nuns' house and see if they have a towel, or something."

"Oh, my! Oh, my! What a mess you all are!" the principal gasped. "Edward, go and take care of the horse and the surrey." She held one of the dripping curls in her hand. "How in the world did this happen?"

"It was one of those automobiles," Cady said.

The principal shook her head. "Well, you can't go to school like this. We will have to find some other clothes for you to wear until we can wash your things."

The mud never came out of the girls' dresses, and their hair ribbons and stockings had to be thrown away. The boys even had mud in their pockets. Oscar and Eliza lay in bed that night, after the children were all asleep, and listened to the rain frogs chirping in the darkness. "Perhaps we should find an easier way for the children to go to school," he said.

"How can we do that?" Eliza asked.

"What do you think about moving to the city?"

"Oh, Oscar, I don't know!" Eliza replied. "We are so settled here. I love Eagle Crest. I would miss it, I'm sure."

"Well then, how about renting a house in the city during the school months?"

Eliza took a deep breath. The rain frogs had stopped singing. Everything was still. "It's something to think about," she whispered.

~ ~ ~ ~

The work at the plantation was especially hard that year. Rains had all but ruined the cotton and turned the cane fields into a sea of mud. The epidemic of yellow fever two years before had taken the lives of some of the workers, and now Oscar felt their absence. Joseph and Isabel had both been ill, and Souri had to stay home and care for them. That left NaNoot and Eliza to manage alone with a house full of children, the oldest thirteen, and the youngest, a two-year-old. When the school year ended, Regina left The Convent and Eagle Crest for a job in the city at a milliner's shop. Eliza and Oscar felt the day Regina left marked the closing of a chapter in their lives together as a family. Eliza also felt Regina was the only one of the children who could calm Oscar down when his temper flared.

"Papa," Edward once asked, "what kind of magic does Regina have over you? She just walks into the room and you calm down."

Oscar often ignored Edward's comments, but this day had been long and he was tired. "There's no magic about it," he said. "When she visits I am glad to see her."

"We should all have that effect on you, right?" Edward replied.

Hilda was born the year Regina left home. Ida immediately took over as the little mother, carrying Hilda around on her hip, feeding her, and playing with her to the exclusion of the other brothers and sisters. Six year old Anna told her mother she was certain Hilda was growing out of Ida's hip.

William

During the summer Edward and his friend William spent a great deal of time in the garden, which had grown considerably larger. During the spring Edward had planted beans and corn, carrots, cucumbers and tomatoes, and even peanuts and watermelon. This year the row of sunflowers was William's job, and as he worked the

104

soil around each giant plant, the flowers seemed to grow larger and larger. Their bright yellow heads soon touched, and each day they all followed the sun together, until dusk.

"Do you think flowers sleep?" William asked Edward one evening as they put away their tools and walked together to the kitchen.

"I don't think so," Edward replied. "I never hear any snoring."

Edward and William shared fishing poles and trips in the surrey to Lafayette to pick up the mail when the train came in. They ate breakfast under the old oak and lunch on the banks of the pond. They sat on the front porch and told stories late into the night, and William told Edward he was his best friend, even though his skin was white.

The talk around the plantation was that William's dog had gone mad. Several of the workers told Oscar they had seen the dog running through the fields with foam dripping from his mouth. The nearest neighbors, John and Mary Mouton rode to Eagle Crest to make certain Eliza understood the danger involved.

"Don't let the children outside, Miss Eliza," John pleaded. "I know it will be hard, but we don't want anyone to get bitten. We saw the dog running in this direction. He is definitely mad and will have to be shot before he bites someone."

Eliza and NaNoot looked at each other, and the fear in their eyes sent Oscar outside to load his rifle. Eliza locked the doors and asked NaNoot to make certain all the children were inside.

Eliza remembered she had sent Ida to the garden, and looking out the kitchen window she saw Oscar and William walking through the backyard. "Oscar!" she called. "We are missing Ida!"

At the sound of her name Ida came from behind the barn, carrying an arm full of vegetables. She walked slowly, smiling at

Oscar and William. Then she stopped. "William!" she called out, "look behind you!"

William turned, and before he could raise his rifle his dog leaped and bit him on the neck. He threw the dog off and began running toward the barn. As the dog stood up, Oscar fired one shot, killing him.

When Jefferson heard what had happened, he held William tightly. "I never thought this would happen to my son, Mr. Oscar. He's such a good boy! I guess I'll go ask Mama to fix a room for him."

Edward helped Joseph and Isabel put thick rolls of cotton all around the little room. They covered the door knobs with cotton too, so William couldn't hurt himself too badly. They covered the floor with old quilts and blankets, and put William's pillow in there so he could rest his head on it if he wanted to. There was no food and no water because he wouldn't be able to drink or eat anyway. William was locked in the room and left to die. Jefferson went to the city and stayed with a friend until Joseph came to tell him that William's cries had stopped. When Jefferson opened the door to the room he found his son dead, with his head on his pillow.

Jefferson buried his only child in a wooden coffin under the old oak. Oscar had a stone marker made, and he and Edward placed it on the fresh mound of dirt. The next spring Edward planted a row of sunflowers along a picket fence which surrounded the grave. When the flowers grew, they were smaller than those in Edward's garden, but they still followed the sun from morning until dusk.

CHAPTER TEN

GEORGE WAS BORN the year Anna started school. By then the sadness surrounding the death of William had eased a little. Edward talked about becoming a teacher, and Jules announced he might like to be a priest one day. Eliza told both of her sons that she thought God was pleased with their choices. However, when Cady informed her father that she was certain she wanted to become a nun, Oscar reacted immediately with a resounding, "No!"

"Why do you want to hide yourself in a convent?" he asked.

Cady could hardly hold back the tears. "I have always wanted to become a nun, Papa. Why do you object to this?"

"Because you are too young to know what you want."

"When will I be old enough?"

Oscar looked at his daughter. Her dark hair fell softly across her shoulders and her blue eyes sparkled beneath long, dark lashes. He shook his head, trying to erase the image of Cady wrapped up in a nun's habit. "You must wait until you are twenty-one years old to make that decision," he said.

Cady discussed Oscar's decision with her mother, but the two eventually agreed there was no way to change his mind. "Why does he feel this way, Mama?" she asked.

"I think he wants a different life for you," Eliza answered. "You will have to wait until you are twenty-one, and pray everyday that he changes his mind and accepts it when you do become a nun."

As the days went by, Cady adjusted to the fact that she must wait and became a second mother to her brothers and sisters, taking over the care of the newest baby, Theresa.

Gabriel

The days at Eagle Crest seemed easy and full of laughter. Oscar often said he felt as though God had blessed the family in a special way. Many of the ordinary family problems seemed to vanish, until Eliza discovered Gabriel had been causing trouble at school.

"But Papa! They started it! I was just defending myself," Gabriel cried out when Oscar confronted him.

"It takes two to make a fight, son!" Oscar replied, glaring at his son.

Gabriel shook his head. "I understand sir, but I didn't start it."

After the third report from the nuns that Gabriel was caught fighting, Oscar decided to send him to the new high school. After Gabriel had attended the school for a month, Oscar saw a strange buggy approaching the house. Seated next to the driver was Gabriel. "Mr. Daigle?" the driver called out. "I am Charles Blake, disciplinarian at Center High School."

"What is the problem, Mr. Blake?" Oscar asked, frowning at his son.

"Your son has been expelled because he tried to fight with the principal. I have been sent to inform you of the incident and to make certain you know he cannot return to Center High."

Oscar stood in stunned silence. "Get down," he told his son, "and go inside the house. Wait for me in the parlor." Oscar turned to Blake. "I apologize for the behavior of my son, although I am not surprised. Please tell the principal I will visit with him tomorrow."

"Certainly Mr. Daigle," Blake replied, "but you must understand the decision is irreversible. He can never return to the school."

Eliza was waiting for Oscar on the porch. "Who was that?" she asked. "And why is Gabriel home from school?"

Oscar looked at Eliza and shook his head. "He has been expelled. He cannot return."

"What will we do?" Eliza whispered. "Where will he go?"

"Let me think for awhile before I decide," Oscar answered.

It was several days before he announced that Gabriel would be joining the Navy. "I have discussed the matter with the naval officials," he said to Gabriel, "and you will report for duty two weeks from tomorrow. Do you understand?"

"Yes, sir," Gabriel answered, "but I am not yet eighteen."

Oscar walked up close to Gabriel and looked steadily at him. "The officials will make an exception in your case, and I think you should be grateful that they are willing to do this," he replied.

When Oscar and Eliza said good-by to Gabriel, Eliza knew she would always remember how young he looked as he boarded the train. She was heartbroken. Edward was already teaching, and Jules was in the seminary. The bitter cold cut through her coat like a knife and she began to shiver. She was expecting another baby soon and Oscar wrapped his arms around her.

"I am very tired," she said. "I want to rest. Let's go home."

The Promise

Eliza's days were linked together by her children, like beads in a necklace, and she found herself faced with not only caring for her children but also watching them leave as they grew up. Eliza was happy when Edward talked about graduation and a job teaching school, but she felt differently about Jules becoming a priest.

"Mama," Jules asked, "do I have your blessing?"

"Of course you do," Eliza replied. "I am afraid I will miss you terribly, though." She put her arms around him and looked into his eyes. "You are the one I can always count on to help," she said. "I think your brothers and sisters look up to you, also."

Each night Eliza knelt with her children to say the rosary. The sounds of prayer filled the room, as each decade of the beads gathered substance from the voices of the children, like wind moving the branches of the trees. "Hail Mary, full of grace." The voice of Jules was a constant over the sniffles and coughs of the children as they rocked back and forth to relieve the pressure on their knees. After all the lanterns had been extinguished, Oscar lay down alongside Eliza and baby Theresa. A full moon had risen, and the room was flooded with pale white light. Oscar fell into a deep sleep and did not awaken when Eliza heard the noise on the front porch.

"What was that?" she whispered. Oscar did not stir. There was another sound, this one more like a scraping noise, and then footsteps. Eliza slipped out of bed and walked close to the open window. She heard voices and saw shadows moving across the porch and down the steps. Leaning slightly she could see several men carrying pieces of firewood from the porch to a buggy waiting under the old oak tree. Eliza reached for Oscar's rifle, and seeing it was loaded she threw open the door with such force that the two men still on the porch dropped the wood and began running. Stepping outside Eliza took aim and fired three shots. The sound echoed, mixing with the cries of the men as they disappeared into the trees.

"Did you see the faces of the wood thieves?" Oscar asked Eliza the next morning.

"No, I did not, she said, "but I think three of them were our workers. I recognized them from the back, which is the way I see them most often in the fields."

Oscar looked at his wife. He had married her when she was seventeen. She had given birth to eleven children, learned to run an entire plantation, and he never knew she could fire a gun.

"I am amazed at you," he said.

"I am amazed at myself!" Eliza laughed.

Oscar shook his head. "Apparently you were not afraid, and that is good. How did you know you could fire a gun?"

"Mama always said God gives you strength when you need it!" Eliza replied.

This whole episode with the wood thieves weighed heavily on Eliza's mind. She was frightened that something like that would happen again and she reminded Oscar of his idea to move to the city. Each time the conversation came up he promised he would find a safe home for his family in Lafayette.

~ ~ ~ ~

On the coldest day of 1914, Mildred was born. Icicles outlined the snow covered roof of Eagle Crest, and life at home for the Daigle family took on a new meaning. Because real snow was a rarity, the roads were closed due to drifts and icy patches, and the children did not have to attend school. Instead of poring over books they sipped steaming soup or gumbo and nibbled on gratons and fried sweet potatoes drizzled with cane syrup. The house was built high off the ground to allow cool air to circulate on hot summer days, but during a winter like this, the cold air collected under the floor and the children hopped around as though they were walking on ice. The only thing to do was crawl into bed, with a warm fire nearby, and listen while Cady told them stories. She set the stage each time by drawing the curtains and extinguishing the lanterns. The children huddled beneath the covers, their eyes shining in the dancing light from the fireplace.

"Once up a time," she began. "TeeToot and Bottom-of-the-pot went for a walk in the woods by the river, and they got lost. Soon it began to get dark.

"Don't worry TeeToot," said Bottom-of-the-pot, "I will find the way home by watching the moon."

"How will that help?" asked TeeToot.

"Because the moon will smile when we are walking in the right direction," said Bottom-of-the-pot.

"But suppose there is no moon tonight," said TeeToot.

"The moon will come along shortly," said Bottom-of-the-pot.

And so the two of them sat on the bank of the river and waited for the moon to rise. It grew darker and darker. Strange sounds began to fill the air. Soon a Fox came walking along and spied the two of them sitting there on the river bank, each eating one of Mama's syrup and peaches sandwiches.

"Hello there," the Fox said, "why are you sitting here? It is almost dark."

"We are waiting for the moon to rise," said TeeToot.

"There will be no moon tonight," said the Fox.

"Oh Bottom," said TeeToot, "we are lost for sure now!"

"I will show you the way home," said the Fox, "but you must give me one of your sandwiches to help me remember the way."

They both handed the Fox one of their sandwiches, and the Fox immediately ate the two sandwiches and then rubbed his head.

"I am beginning to remember the way," the Fox said, "but I need at least one more sandwich to help me."

TeeToot took his last sandwich and handed it to the Fox.

After the Fox ate the sandwich he said, "Come on, I will show you the way."

He led them along the river bank to the edge of a swamp, and then he said, "Give me another sandwich and I will take you all the way home."

Bottom-of-the-pot had only one sandwich left and so he told the Fox, "I don't want to give you any more sandwiches and you have just eaten TeeToot's last one. We should be home by now, don't you think?"

"Do you live on the edge of this swamp?" the Fox asked.

"No," they both said.

"Do you have any more sandwiches?" the Fox asked.

"No," they both said again.

"Then I can't help you," said the Fox, and with that he left.

TeeToot and Bottom-of-the-pot walked back to the river and sat on the bank again. They fell asleep, and the moon rose high in the sky, making everything bright as day. Living in a hole on the river bank was a big Nutria, and he came out and saw TeeToot and Bottom-of-the-pot asleep. He sniffed their fingers and smelled the syrup and peaches sandwiches.

"Wake up," said the Nutria. "Why are you asleep out here on the river bank?"

"We are lost," said TeeToot.

113

"I will take you home," said the Nutria," if you give me one of your syrup and peaches sandwiches."

Bottom-of-the-pot looked very closely at the Nutria and said, "I did not know nutria ate sandwiches."

The Nutria looked very closely at Bottom-of-the-pot and said, "Yes, we need syrup and peaches sandwiches to help our brains remember things like the way home in the dark."

"Wait a minute," said TeeToot, "it is not dark anymore. Look Bottom, we can see the house."

TeeToot threw a stick at the Nutria and watched it run back into his hole. Then TeeToot and Bottom-of-the-pot ran all the way home and sat at the kitchen table, and together they ate the last syrup and peaches sandwich."

"Why would someone be named Bottom-of-the-pot?" Armand asked.

Cady tried to answer without laughing. "Because that's what he looked like!"

"No," replied Armand, "you are just making that up!"

"What!" Anna gasped. "Cady makes things up?"

Oscar sat up in bed and listened. He could hear laughter and a few shrieks. "Cher! Are the children still telling stories?"

Eliza smiled in the darkness. "Why yes," she said, "I believe they are."

"Don't you think it is time for bed?"

"They cannot get to school until it stops snowing," she answered. "Leave them alone. They will probably fall asleep soon."

CHAPTER ELEVEN

THE YEAR LYDIA was born marked the opening of a brand new hotel in Lafayette. Once a day, Little Willie's Bus brought people to and from the hotel and the train station. The hotel even had a restaurant, and when the four o'clock whistle blew at the end of the work day, the politicians gathered there, filling the air with cigar smoke and laughter. Opposite the hotel was a garage which sold automobiles, and next to the garage was a pharmacy, then a bank, and a soda fountain with a candy shop. A person could visit the dressmaker or the tailor shop, then walk to the grocery store or the dry goods shop and not have traveled more than a couple of city blocks.

Ida left Eagle Crest to teach school and attend college and Cady became the sole "Nanny" for eight brothers and sisters. Although she was two years away from turning twenty-one, she did not attempt to discuss becoming a nun with Oscar again. Oscar kept his promise and made arrangements to rent a house in Lafayette which was so close to The Convent that the children could walk.

"I know this is the right thing to do," Eliza said, "but I will miss Eagle Crest."

"There will be less danger for you and the children in the city," Oscar replied. "There will be no more wood thieves in the middle of the night and we can return to Eagle Crest each summer."

~ ~ ~ ~

"Why, I never dreamed I would have a chance to use one of these," Eliza whispered as she ran her hand over the telephone which hung on the wall in the hallway of the house in Lafayette.

"Papa," Lucille said, "why didn't you tell us there was a telephone here?"

Oscar held the receiver to his ear. "It's broken. There is no sound coming out."

"It is not broken," Anna whispered to Lucille. "He just doesn't know how to use it."

Anna tapped the lever on the phone and a voice asked, "Number please?"

"See?" she said. "It does too work."

Armand raced through the front door crying out, "There are no bathrooms outside!"

"Come here," Oscar said as he opened the door to the hall bathroom and turned on the light.

Armand looked inside. "We have some of those lights at school," he said. He looked around the bathroom and pointing to the toilet, said, "We have one of those at school, too!"

"Papa," Lucille said again, "someone told us there was a movie theater downtown. Is that true?"

"Yes," he said. "Why?"

"Oh, Papa! We must go to see a movie there!"

"We did not move here to visit the movie house," he answered.

"But there is so much to do and see here," Lucille sighed. "Why can't we live here forever, and never go back, not even for the summer?"

"Mama," Anna called from the door which led to the kitchen. "There is a little bedroom here, next to the back door. Who will sleep there?"

"That room is for Souri," Eliza answered.

Anna studied the tiny bedroom. The single bed was covered with a blue blanket, and there were two white pillows against the headboard. Another little pillow covered with blue lace nested between the white ones. At the foot of the bed there was a white chest painted with red roses, and on the table next to the bed was a lamp painted with roses, and an empty picture frame. The room had a little window with red and blue panes, and a lace curtain pulled to one side with a string of red beads. Across from the bed was a door which led to Souri's bathroom."

"Oh, she has her own bathroom," Anna whispered. "How lucky can one person get!"

Souri arrived shortly after everyone had moved into their respective rooms. The children greeted her with cheers and immediate requests for something to eat and drink.

"I don't think Miss Eliza wants you to spoil your supper," Souri replied. "Y'all go on now. The adults have things to do!"

After supper Oscar called the children out on to the wide front porch. There were signs of fall everywhere. Leaves made a blanket across the front lawn, and the flowers which had bloomed so faithfully all summer looked as though they were asleep. The heat of the day disappeared quickly once the sun went down, and the wind blew from the north instead of the south. It was drier now, and without the rain the crickets and tree frogs didn't have much to sing about. Oscar lit his pipe and leaned back in a rocker.

"I want all of you to understand that you must listen to your mother while I am away during the day. She is in charge, and you

117

must help her and Souri with this house. It is ours for as long as we wish, but we must take good care of it."

"Where will you sleep, Papa?" Armand asked.

"I will be here with your mother as much as possible," he answered. "But during the harvest I will probably spend many nights at Eagle Crest. Then it will be very important that you obey your mother because I will not be here to spank you!"

Anna stood up and walked up to Oscar. "Papa," she whispered, "there is something I forgot to do before I left Eagle Crest."

"What is it?" Oscar asked.

"I can't tell you until I go back with you to Eagle Crest. Please say that you will take me back soon."

"Is it that important?"

"Yes, Papa," Anna replied. "It is."

Oscar looked at his daughter. "I'll discuss this with your mother," he said, and then taking Eliza's hand he kissed it. "Cher, here we are in the city at last. Do you like the house?"

"It's a beautiful house," she replied. "I feel we will be happy here."

"You know, not only will the children be able to walk to school, they will also be able to walk to the college."

Oscar rocked in silence, puffing on his pipe and humming softly. "Cher," he finally said, "I have always wanted to go to college."

For a moment she didn't know what to say. She wondered if this was something recent, or had he always felt this way?

"Why don't you go to college if that is what you want?" she said.

"I don't think I can, at least not right now," Oscar answered. "I have to take care of the plantation, and that is a full time job."

"Don't you think Joseph and Jefferson could manage the workers?"

"Perhaps," Oscar replied. "But I am not ready to have someone else manage Eagle Crest."

The trees cast their unmoving patterns in a black mosaic on the porch floor. Somewhere down the street a dog was barking, and the faint sound of voices drifted from across the street. The neighbors were sitting on their front porch also.

CHAPTER TWELVE

AFTER ROSE WAS born there were ten children living in the house which Oscar rented in Lafayette. Although life was much easier now, Oscar missed the familiar sounds and smells of Eagle Crest. He thought about his mother often. After his father Francois died, Leocade became both father and mother. She would not have moved to the city because her freedom to live as she wished was at the center of her being. To Oscar she was strong and decisive, riding through life with great determination, just as she rode her horses. When her stable boy, Samuel B. Cross rode one of Leocade's horses into town, Oscar knew something had happened to his mother.

"She's gone, Mr. Oscar. She's gone." Samuel sobbed. "I just don't know what we gonna do. She wasn't even feeling poorly, and now she's gone."

"Where did you find her," Oscar asked, his eyes filled with tears.

"In the stable, Mr. Oscar, next to the feed buckets." Samuel replied. "She must have finished taking the saddle off Southern Belle and looked like she was fixing to feed her."

"Did you call someone?"

"Yes, sir. I called the doctor. He came right away, but it was too late."

After the funeral mass, Mister and Southern Belle pulled the coffin to the graveyard, where Father Richard said the final prayers for their mistress. The winter air was clear and cool. Most of the trees had lost their leaves and the sidewalks and streets were littered with patches of red and gold. Oscar and his brothers sat in silence on the front porch of Oscar's house. Inside, Eliza and Souri were setting out food. Music drifted from the phonograph in the parlor. As friends and members of the family walked up the steps leading to the front door, they stopped and gave their condolences.

"Your mother was a jewel," they said. "She was someone you could always count on. She had courage and strength. She was solid as a rock."

Oscar knew better. His mother was as free as the wind, happy with herself and the world around her. She would not like to be called a jewel, because she was not that. She was the setting which kept the jewel from getting lost, from falling out of the place it was meant to be. She did have courage and strength, but she was not always a rock. She could be soft, like the rain when it falls as mist across the prairies. She loved passionately, and demanded much of herself and others. And she was honest with life. She died where she wanted to die, closest to her horses. They were like her heart. They took her all the places she ever wanted to go.

Oscar brought Mister and Southern Belle to live at Eagle Crest with the other horses, so he could ride them when he went to the plantation each week. Joseph and Jefferson had become able supervisors, and between the two of them, the fences were mended and the barn and stable repaired without Oscar's help. It was only during harvest time that Oscar felt he should supervise the work and he often asked Eliza to go with him.

"Anna, come here please," Eliza called out. "I am going with Papa to Eagle Crest for the afternoon. You will have to help Souri with the children."

Anna caught her breath. "Oh, Papa! Remember I asked you if I could go with you to Eagle Crest! Oh, please Papa. There is

121

something I have to do. Something I forgot, and now it is more important than ever."

"What is this thing you have forgotten to do?" Oscar asked.

"I can't tell you, but it is something I cannot do here. Oh, please let me come with you and Mama."

"What do you think?" Eliza asked Oscar. "Should we bring her with us?"

"I suppose it can't hurt," he replied. "Besides, I am very curious about this request."

The distance between the house in the city and Eagle Crest had grown shorter as the city grew larger. The roads were crowded with bicycles, buggies and even a few automobiles. When Oscar saw one of those he commented how foolish it was to feed the automobile expensive gasoline instead of feeding a good horse a little bit of hay.

~ ~ ~ ~

Anna stood up in the surrey as it stopped next to the front porch of Eagle Crest. "Where is Mama's horse?" she asked. Oscar pointed to the back pasture where Crescent grazed alone. "She looks lonely, Papa," she said. "Why is she by herself?"

"She is so small that sometimes the bigger horses bully her," Oscar answered.

Anna shook her head. "I think you are wrong. I know Crescent. I have ridden her at least three times a week since I was old enough to ride. She likes people, and she likes to be ridden often." Anna jumped from the surrey and began running to the back pasture.

"Where are you going?" Oscar called out.

Anna turned around and, running backwards, she yelled, "I need to ride Crescent. I forgot to do that before I left. I promised her I would ride her one last time!"

"What about a saddle?" Oscar called out again.

"Don't need one!" she replied.

By the time Oscar and Eliza walked to the pond, Anna was riding Crescent bareback, at a full gallop across the pastures. She gripped the horse with her legs, and holding on to the mane, Anna rode through clouds of brown dust. Her hair sparkled in the sunlight, and as Oscar watched he thought for a moment his mother was in the saddle instead.

"Cher, I did not know Anna could ride like that!"

"She does ride well," Eliza replied. "I wonder where she gets that from."

In two years, Anna was sixteen and out of high school. She began teaching right away in a little town near Côte Gelée.

Cady turned twenty-one, and went off to become a nun. By this time, Oscar had accepted the fact that his oldest daughter was determined to "give her life to God," just as she said she would.

Summers at Eagle Crest

At the end of each school year, Eliza brought the children back to Eagle Crest for the summer. All those days spent in the classroom evaporated, like bubbles in the sunlight. They rode horses, climbed in the hayloft, ran across the pastures, chased the chickens, and threw each other down in the soft grass under the old oak tree. The workers still picked cotton in the moonlight and cut the rippling waves of sugar cane, piling the wagons full for the trip into town. Isabel still cooked the noon meal and, if it rained, the workers still looked for the rainbow over the barn. It was easy for the boys to forget about the things the city had to offer when all a person really needed was a soft bed of grass and a cloud or two to make pictures. The girls thought differently however, and the city called out to them from time to time.

"Armand," Lucille said, "I need to go into Lafayette to buy some things. Mama said you would be able to take me."

Armand looked at his sister. She was wearing her best blue dress, the one with the red ribbons on the shoulders. She had on a matching bonnet and gloves, and was carrying a parasol. Mmm, he thought, that doesn't look like a going-shopping outfit to me.

"And where would a store be selling some things today?" he asked.

"Oh, don't be silly, Armand," she replied. "You know what I mean!"

"Are you asking me to drive the surrey into town so that you can shop?"

Lucille narrowed her eyes. "Yes," she said slowly, making a hissing sound.

"You are not asking properly."

"Oh! I don't think I can stand any more of this!" Lucille cried out. "Please take me! Is that what you want, a please?"

"You don't have to yell," he whispered. "I'll just go and check this out with Mama."

Before taking his place in the driver's seat, Armand actually helped Lucille into the surrey. She sat in the back, her blue dress spread across the seat like a frilly blanket. Armand noticed her bonnet was tied under her chin with a red ribbon which matched those on her shoulders. The ride through the gates of Eagle Crest and down past the cane field was uneventful until suddenly the

124

horse reared up, and bolted in the opposite direction. Armand never knew whether there was a snake in the road, or the horse decided to turn around on his own and go home. At first Armand held on to the edges of the surrey. The horse was running wild with Lucille shrieking in the back seat. The surrey hit a rock, and bounced Armand out onto the side of the road, and the last view he had of Lucille was a blur of red ribbons, a bonnet flying in the wind, and her blue dress blowing up across her face as the horse ran for his life, back to Eagle Crest.

When Armand walked into the parlor, Eliza was waiting for him. Lucille had vanished into her bedroom. He could hear her sobbing.

"Tell me what happened," Eliza asked.

"I'm not sure," Armand said. "The horse must have been spooked by something. He turned and ran as though his tail was on fire."

"Did you try to stop him?"

"I didn't think I could. I just held on until the surrey hit something and I fell out!"

"Lucille said you were laughing the whole time. Is this true?"

"Oh, Mama," Armand said, "in one second she was out of sight. How could she possibly know if I was laughing or crying?"

~ ~ ~ ~

In two years Armand left home to become a teacher and Florence was born, fulfilling the prophecy of Edward that the women would permanently outnumber the men in the family. Unfortunately, Florence cried a lot and Eliza was often exhausted after trying to keep her happy. Although Anna had moved away,

125

she often dropped by unannounced to help Eliza with the younger children.

The morning after a particularly bad night with Florence, Anna offered to try to calm her little sister down. She wrapped Florence tightly in a blanket and walked out into the yard, humming and rocking her gently in her arms. She wondered what her own child would be like, and would the father of her baby love her madly, or just a little bit? She thought about all the things she loved to do. Ride horses. Teach school. Talk to her friends endlessly, about life, and all the different paths a person could take to find happiness. How many boyfriends would she have, and would they be rich, or "poor as church mice," as her mother would say.

Eliza watched Anna from a window and realized she had more than one daughter who was good with children. Just a few months before, a woman shopping in Sognier's dry goods store stopped her to ask about Ida. "I am Marie LeBlanc's mother," the woman said. "My daughter was a student of Miss Ida. When Marie was a senior and preparing for graduation, we could not afford to buy a white dress for the ceremony. Miss Ida bought my daughter a dress, shoes, and stockings for her graduation, and refused to accept any amount of money from us to help pay for Marie's clothes. Marie looked beautiful, and we will never forget your daughter's generosity."

~ ~ ~ ~

During the summer Eliza felt the absence of the older children who had moved away, especially Gabriel who had been in the Navy four years when World War I ended. Eliza had not seen him since the day he left. He wrote to his mother frequently though,

126

and most of the time mentioned his numerous visits to the brig. Oscar had a good laugh over his letters, commenting that even the Navy couldn't straighten him out.

When Eliza heard a knock on the front door of Eagle Crest she opened it without thinking. Gabriel was standing there, in his uniform and smiling. "Mama," he said, "I've missed you! Did you get my letters?"

"Yes, of course I did," Eliza said, tears streaming down her cheeks. "I've kept them all."

Gabriel looked around. "Where's Papa?"

"He and George have gone to town. He'll be back soon. He will be surprised to see you, son."

Gabriel saw four little faces looking from behind the bedroom door. "Who are these pretty little girls?" he asked.

"You have been gone a long time," Eliza answered. "This is Rose, and Lydia, and Mildred, and Theresa."

"Are these my little sisters?"

"Yes, and there is another one, Florence. She is asleep. Now tell me, how did you know to come to Eagle Crest? We could have been at our house in Lafayette."

"I didn't know that!" Gabriel replied, shaking his head. "The Navy brought me here in one of those new automobiles. I have been gone a long time!"

Gabriel walked into the parlor and sat down. He closed his eyes, and tried to guess what Souri was cooking. A pork roast, maybe. He thought he could smell baked sweet potatoes too, filled with butter and cane syrup. He heard the sound of the surrey pulling up to the porch, and looking at Eliza he quickly stood up when he saw his father in the doorway.

127

"Gabriel," Oscar said. "When did you get in?" He shook his son's hand, and then embraced him as though the past four years had never existed.

At the end of the week, the same automobile arrived back at Eagle Crest. "I have decided to stay in the Navy to teach the new recruits," Gabriel said as he prepared to leave. "Looks like you will have one more teacher in the family!"

Oscar put his arm around Eliza and the two of them watched their son leave once again. "Who would have thought he could make such a good career out of such a bad past!" Oscar said.

~ ~ ~ ~

It was August now and the air was so still the trees seemed to be painted on the sky. Oscar and Joseph had gone to town. The late afternoon light suddenly turned into darkness, and the wind began to rustle the leaves and grass. Eliza walked outside. At first there was only a slight rain, then slowly the sky grew heavy with clouds racing to the north. In the distance, there was a strange rumble, like a train starting out of the station.

Eliza ran inside and called the children together. "All of you get into the middle of the house. Hurry now, there isn't much time."

As Eliza and the children huddled together, she began to pray. Soon the words of the prayers were drowned in the sounds of the storm. The rain fell with such fury that the children held their ears and cried out, "Mama! Mama! Make it stop!" Eliza tried to wrap her arms around them. "Pray, children. Pray! God will take care of us." The old oak groaned as its limbs twisted and turned in the wind. "Are we going to die?" Mildred asked, pressing against Theresa and Lydia. "God will take care of us," Eliza said again.

When the wind stopped screaming, Eliza stood up. There was an eerie silence throughout the house. Everything seemed to be in place until she walked into the kitchen. A large branch had broken one of the windows, and the force of the wind and rain had soaked the kitchen walls. A calendar hanging near the back door lay strewn across the floor, and next to it was a small piece of paper which Eliza recognized immediately. Many years before Edward promised to pay his father back for helping him plant a garden. That promise was written in an IOU note for money which was tacked to the frame of the kitchen door. Eliza dried the note with her dress and stuck it back on the door with the tack which still rested in the wood.

Looking out the broken window, she could see the golden light from the setting sun streaming through the holes in the clouds. "Stay here," she told the children as she walked outside. The old oak had lost most of its leaves, and the fruit trees were bare. Only part of the barn was still standing, and the horses and cattle were grazing together in the back yard.

"George, come here," she called, "one of the cows is loose in the back pasture."

"What was that?" he asked, looking at the branches piled against the porch.

"A tornado, perhaps," Eliza replied. "I wonder if your father is on his way here."

When Oscar and Joseph returned a little after dark they took lanterns and walked across the field to the row of houses where the workers lived. Jefferson met his father and Oscar. "I thought I would die," he said. "I couldn't walk outside cause of the rain and wind. Couldn't even see!"

Dawn broke with a clear blue sky. The damage to Eagle Crest was not much more than a few bare trees and broken fences, and a barn with only one side. Oscar and Joseph rounded up the horses and cattle, and the workers combed the soggy grass for the fruit which had blown off the trees. The sugar cane was flattened, but soon the heat of the sun made the cane stand tall again. Strangely enough the cotton crop survived best of all.

"Were you frightened by the storm, Cher?" Oscar asked Eliza.

"I would be lying if I told you no," she answered. "But I do strongly believe God will always take care of us, and He did."

"Do you think you would be better in the city during a storm?"

Eliza took a deep breath. "I think that a storm frightens me more in the country. Help seems so far away. But," she continued, "it is not just the storm. Everything is harder at Eagle Crest. In the city we have running water and electricity. There are stores nearby, and neighbors to help us." Eliza heard her own words and remembered what her mother told her about living in a house in the middle of nowhere.

Oscar looked at his wife. "Cher, would you like your own house in the city?"

"Oh, Oscar, is that possible?" Eliza said.

"I have often thought about building a new house for you," he answered. "If I can buy the land I am thinking of, then I will build that house."

CHAPTER THIRTEEN

OSCAR BOUGHT THE land next door to the house he rented. It was nearly five acres, with enough room for fruit trees, a garden, and a smokehouse. The back part of the land could be used as a pasture for some of the horses from Eagle Crest. Each morning, after the older children left for school, Eliza looked at the land from her bedroom window. She knew exactly where her new house would sit, a little back from the street to give plenty of room for the front porch. She wanted her bedroom to open on the porch with a long window all the way to the floor. The front of the house would also have a bay, with three windows, just like a house she once saw. I'll ask Oscar to put a sidewalk all around the house, she thought, and I'll plant roses next to the sidewalk, and maybe even some bridal wreath by the back door.

Oscar and Eliza walked across the land often, telling each other their dreams for the house. Along one side, four young camphor trees grew in a straight line.

"Whoever planted those trees did a good job," Eliza said.

"I'm not sure they were planted there," Oscar replied. "I think they are volunteers."

Eliza laughed. "That's really what life is all about, isn't it? Most successful people are volunteers. They trust in God and give life a try, and they don't expect too much in return."

"That's pretty philosophical," he said. "Do you believe that?"

"Yes," she replied. "I do."

Idea Landry waved as she walked with Pierre and Julie across the front yard. This was one of her regular visits which were more

131

frequent now that Eliza lived in the city. "This is beautiful land!" she said. "When will you start to build?"

"I want to wait until I am certain I have enough money," Oscar replied.

"Such fine land," she said, "surely you can mortgage it."

Oscar shook his head. "I am not willing to mortgage the land."

Idea looked at her son-in-law. His responsible attitude surprised her and she nodded in agreement. Anna and Lucille were the first to greet their grandmother when the children returned from school. "Why, you are all grown up," Idea said. "When did you do that?"

The girls laughed. "Oh, Grandma," Lucille said, "we just look older. We really aren't!"

"Must be that makeup," Pierre snickered.

"Yes," Oscar answered. "Let me tell you a little story about that makeup."

"Aw, come on, Papa," Lucille cried out. "I won't do that again."

"This story should be a good one," Pierre whispered to Julie.

Oscar leaned over and looked at Idea. "You see, I made a terrible mistake. I allowed Lucille and Anna to have a charge account at the City Pharmacy. Yesterday, I received the bill, which was itemized. Powder and Rouge. Powder and Rouge. Five purchases of makeup in three weeks. Very expensive. Too expensive! Lucille bought most of it."

"But Papa," Lucille said, "you said we could charge there."

"That was to be only in an emergency," Oscar replied.

Pierre laughed. "That was an emergency," he said. "Look at that face!"

~ ~ ~ ~

As Eliza helped her mother climb into the buggy, Idea handed her an envelope and told her to open it later, after everyone had gone to bed. After supper, when all the lights were turned off, Eliza sat in her rocker, and with the light from the street lamp she opened the envelope. Inside was enough money to build her house.

Three Carpenters

Oscar found three men who claimed they were carpenters and had references. One of the men was older and said he knew how to frame a house and would supervise the job.

"Mr. Dugas," Oscar asked, "who are your references?"

"Oh, Mr. Daigle, please call me Claude," Dugas replied. "Here, I have a list of people I have done work for."

Oscar glanced over the list. "I will contact these people and let you know by the end of the week," he said. Oscar was not able to locate three of the people on the list. The fourth name was a man called Robert Cormier, the owner of the restaurant near the Pinhook Bridge. When Oscar arrived at the restaurant, he was cleaning the windows.

"Good day, Mr. Cormier," Oscar called out. "How are you today?"

"A little good. A little bad," he answered. "And what brings you here?"

"I want to know if Claude Dugas has ever done work for you?"

"Yes, he has," Robert answered. "Are you building something?"

"I am trying to find reputable carpenters to build a house for my family. He gave me your name."

"Well, I would say Claude is all right," Robert said, "but when he worked for me he had a man working with him who was not worth anything. In fact he cost me money!"

"Did Claude supervise the work?"

"No, actually he and this idiot did the work. I ended up having to pay them both, of course, and the stupid one should have been sent to jail!"

Oscar shook his head. "What went wrong, if you don't mind my asking?"

Robert motioned for Oscar to follow him as he walked to the front of the building. "Look well at the front door," he said. "Do you see anything?"

Oscar studied the door. "It may be the afternoon light, but it looks as though one side of the door is larger than the other."

"That is not the light," Robert said. "One side of the door is larger because one side of the door frame is higher. That door was framed wrong and the whole front of the building is off about two inches. Every window and door is cockeyed!"

Oscar left the restaurant with a bad feeling in the pit of his stomach. Unfortunately, there were no other carpenters in the entire city, and he knew he would have to settle for Claude Dugas and his helpers.

~ ~ ~ ~

Dugas and his men began work on the first Monday in February, in 1920. The lumber was delivered on time, and Claude and Oscar went over the drawings of the house together. The two men actually got along, and Eliza was hopeful that building the house would not be a problem. At first Claude did most of the work.

134

Once the spring rains arrived however, the situation changed. If it was raining in the morning, Claude did not show up at all, and the two helpers often did. Unsupervised, they made mistakes which Oscar caught and forced them to correct.

"Can't you see that corner is not square?" Oscar called out.

The two helpers by now were working on another corner. "We'll go back to that one in a minute," one of them called back. "Yea, soon as we finish this one!" the other added.

Eliza joined Oscar as he watched the men working. "Maybe you should tell those men to wait until Claude comes back," she said.

"Then we will never finish this!" he replied. "It's already been three months. I have called Claude Dugas repeatedly, and he does not return my calls. I will not pay these men, or Claude for that matter until most of this is built."

Eventually, Claude did return, and the work went more smoothly. Soon the entire house was framed and it was time for the roof. Oscar was relieved. "At least we've gotten this far," he mumbled to himself. He had been careful to pay Claude and his carpenters when they finished large sections of the frame. On the day Claude asked Oscar to pay him for the roof, he also gave Oscar a list of supplies needed to finish the house.

"Where did you get these prices?" Oscar asked him.

"That's what it will take to finish up, Mr. Daigle," Claude answered.

"I can't afford this!" Oscar shot back.

Claude shook his head. "These are the best prices I can get. Everything has gone up during this year."

"You and your men will have to stop working until I find more money to finish the house," Oscar answered and then turned and walked away.

When Eliza and the children returned to Eagle Crest for the summer, Oscar stayed behind and vowed he would finish the house alone if necessary. Many times he sat on the front porch of the rent house, smoking his pipe, a thousand thoughts filling his mind. He looked at the new house. It was beautiful, even as a skeleton of what it was supposed to be. He traced the parlor and the bedrooms with his eyes. He could see the upstairs and the odd corner that was never fixed. No one will ever know, he thought. He could see where he was going to put the sidewalk, and where Eliza would put her sewing machine, and where they would sit at the long table, for all the meals the future would bring. Were those children playing inside, or was it just the wind? Is that light a reflection from the mirror on Eliza's dressing table, or is it simply the sunlight?

"Papa, what are you doing out here?" Edward asked as he stepped onto the porch. "Is Mama still here?"

Oscar stood up and shook his son's hand. "Edward, it's good to see you. You just missed your mother. She and the children have gone to Eagle Crest."

"So why are you sitting out here?"

Oscar pointed to the new house. "Look, we are almost finished."

"Looks great!" Edward replied. "What's next?"

Oscar did not answer. Edward looked at his father carefully. "I can tell something is wrong. What is it?"

Oscar handed the list of supplies to Edward. "This is what it will take to finish the house."

Edward stared at the piece of paper. "This is quite a lot of money, isn't it?"

Oscar nodded.

"Do you have the money?" Edward asked.

Oscar shook his head no.

"What will you do?" Edward asked again.

"I don't know," Oscar answered.

Edward suggested the two of them go to Eagle Crest to discuss the situation with Eliza. "Let's take my automobile," he said, "and I'll bring you back in the morning."

The two men rode in silence, each one swallowed by their own thoughts. Oscar could not believe he had run out of money after he had been so careful. What would he tell Eliza?

She listened as Oscar told her what had happened. "Let me see the list," she said. "Is all of this necessary?"

"I'm afraid so," he replied. "The materials have almost doubled in price, and the roof took the last of the money."

~ ~ ~ ~

Edward sat at the little table in the kitchen while Eliza and Souri fixed supper. He tried to remember what he felt as a child wrapped snugly in the arms of Eagle Crest. His eyes roamed the old room, resting first on the wood stove and then on the IOU note, still pinned to the frame of the back door. Without saying a word he took the note, and looking to see whether it was still legible, he slipped it into his pocket.

When he brought his father back to the city, Oscar was no closer to a solution. "I do not want to borrow money," he said, "but I may have to do that."

137

"The problem with borrowing money is that you have to pay it back," Edward said.

Oscar rubbed his forehead. "I want to have a house for your mother which is free from debt. I will have to find another way."

"Can you sell some of the land around Eagle Crest?" Edward asked.

"I've thought of that, but it may take too long. The house can't sit there, unfinished."

Before he left, Edward walked around the new house with Oscar. He rubbed his hand over the pocket with the IOU note, as though the note was speaking to him. He remembered the day he initialed it as a seven-year-old boy and he wondered if his father remembered it also.

The Traiteur

Not long after Eliza and the children arrived at Eagle Crest, three-year-old Lydia became ill. At first the symptoms were mild. She cried a lot and rubbed her head, and when Eliza pressed her own cheek to the baby's forehead Lydia's skin felt very hot.

"Souri," Eliza called, "come here."

"Oh, Miss Eliza," Souri said. "That baby's sick! Poor little thing, just look at those red cheeks."

Eliza mopped Lydia's skin with wet towels, and tried to get her to drink some water. Lydia's fever went higher that night, and to make matters worse, Eagle Crest was enveloped in a summer thunderstorm.

"Miss Eliza, let me get the traiteur," Souri said.

"I don't know, Souri," Eliza answered. "Do you really think he can help?"

"I think so," she said, "and anyway, soon as this storm stops we can go for the doctor."

Wrapped in a burlap sack, Souri walked across the field, past the old oak, toward the row of houses where the workers lived. The thunder rolled across the sky, sending long, wide fingers of lightening through the tree tops. Eliza lost Souri in the darkness, and walking back to Lydia's little bed, she picked up the baby and began to pray. After what seemed an eternity, the front door opened and Souri walked in with the traiteur.

He looked down at Lydia as he placed both of his hands on her head. Shutting his eyes he whispered, "In the name of the Father, and of the Son, and of the Holy Ghost. Amen." After that, only his lips moved and no one could hear what he was saying. He paused, and pulled a handful of leaves from his coat pocket. Placing the leaves on Lydia's forehead, he continued his prayers. He again reached into his pocket and this time he pulled out a long string, which he blessed and then studied it in the light of the bedroom lantern. The string was thick and had nine knots in it. As he tied the string around Lydia's head, he recited nine prayers. Once he finished the prayers, he left as quickly as he had come.

The baby was so still that Eliza placed her hand on her stomach to make certain she was still breathing.

"Did you tell Joseph to go for the doctor in the morning?" she asked Souri.

"I surely did, and he said he would go before morning, if the storm quits."

Sometime during the early morning the wind and rain stopped, and not long after, Dr. Gilbert arrived. He examined Lydia careful-ly, removing the leaves from her forehead. "She may have a touch of yellow fever," he said. "Even though the last epidemic was years ago we still see cases from time to time, especially in the summer."

"Will she be all right?" Eliza asked.

"I think so," he replied. "She's so little that she will not have too many symptoms other than fever. Try to get her to drink some water and keep her skin cool with wet towels. She should feel better in a couple of days."

"What about the string around her head?"

Dr. Gilbert laughed. "That's a curing string, and I'm a little reluctant to remove it. It can't hurt to leave it in place. You just never know about these things."

~ ~ ~ ~

Edward paid another visit to Eagle Crest at the end of the summer. Finding Oscar and Eliza on the porch, he waved and then reached into his coat pocket. "Mama, Papa I have something for you," Edward said. He pulled out an envelope which he handed to his father.

Oscar opened the envelope and held up a small piece of paper which was brown and wrinkled with age, the writing barely legible: "I owe my papa money for farm work, signed E D."

Oscar looked at his son. "You remembered this?" he asked, shaking his head and handing the note to Eliza. "See Edward's initials there, he was only seven when he signed this."

"There's more Papa!" Edward said.

Oscar lifted money out of the envelope, enough money to finish the house, enough for the dream to come true. Edward put his hand on his father's shoulder. "It is the payment I owe you for teaching me how to grow a garden, and how to live. Besides it is also a gift to Mama. Now she can have her own house in the city."

"Edward, is this money you have saved?" Eliza asked. "Are you certain you want to give this to us?"

"Take it Mama," he answered. "I may not have it later. There is something else I want to tell you. I am going to marry the most beautiful girl in the world, besides you, of course!"

The next morning, Edward drove Oscar to Lafayette where he called Claude Dugas and told him to finish the house. By the end of the day, Dugas and his two helpers were already measuring the front of the house for the porch.

"Mr. Daigle, do you want the front porch to stop at that bay, or go around it?" Dugas asked.

Oscar looked at him carefully. "I don't think I have ever seen a porch go around a bay, have you, Mr. Dugas?"

"Well, maybe once," he replied.

"No, Mr. Dugas. I do not want the porch to go around the bay. I want the porch to stop at the bay. Do you understand?"

"Oh, certainly sir, certainly! Stop at the bay. What about the other side?"

Oscar took a deep breath. "Just build the front porch, Mr. Dugas, and make it look like a front porch."

"Can he make it go around the bay?" Edward whispered.

"He will probably try," Oscar whispered, "and then I will have to kill him."

"I can see the problem," Edward said, clearing his throat and trying not to laugh.

Once the exterior was finished, Dugas and his helpers turned their attention to the inside of the house. Before long, Eliza was able to walk down the hall and look into the bedrooms. She

141

stepped into the parlor, with its bay windows overlooking the front yard and College Avenue, and watched the automobiles and buggies go by. When she stood in the kitchen and looked out the back windows she could see the wide pastures behind the house. Room enough for fruit trees and horses, she thought. Next to the dining room there was a place for her sewing machine, near a door which led to the side yard and the camphor trees. This was where Oscar told Dugas to build a small smokehouse and a potato shed. It was here, also, that he envisioned a garden like the one he and Edward had planted many years before at Eagle Crest.

The year was fast drawing to a close. Oscar announced that he was certain by next spring they would be in the new house. Eliza welcomed the news because she was pregnant again, and at forty-five years of age she felt certain this would be the last baby.

NaNoot with the Green Eyes

The New Year began with the birth of Lloyd. When Eliza saw NaNoot walk through the door, she sighed in relief that her old friend and midwife would be with her at least one more time. Lloyd's birth proved to be a difficult one, and although Eliza did not complain, she said afterwards that she felt her age.

NaNoot examined her patient very carefully. "You don't look well, Miss Eliza," she said. "You must take more than six weeks to recover; otherwise you won't be any good to anyone!"

"Will you stay a little while longer?" Eliza asked her.

"Yes, child," she replied, "as long as you need me to stay."

Eliza turned her head and stared at the crib. "Do you think this will be my last child?"

"I don't know," NaNoot said. "Only God knows such things."

During her time spent resting after Lloyd's birth, Eliza often studied her friend NaNoot as she moved about the house. Eliza noticed she had grown older, although her green eyes still sparkled. She always wore her hair pulled back and tied with a ribbon, but once, Eliza saw her hair down, falling softly across her shoulders in wide, loose curls. It was the color of wheat and Eliza wondered how it had happened that NaNoot was Mulatto and her brother Joseph was so dark that he could disappear on a moonless night.

Once Eliza asked Oscar this question and he replied, "She had a mother who was beautiful with green eyes and long blond hair. Joseph saw her once, and someone told him that his father met her in New Orleans."

Eliza shook her head. "Joseph's mother was obviously not the same woman, but she accepted NaNoot and raised her as one of her own. Why is that?"

"I can't say for sure," Oscar told her, "but I think that this kind of thing was pretty common back then. Still is, in fact."

For Eliza, discussions about family secrets often brought thoughts about Regina and a nagging question. What will happen to the family when Regina's secret is revealed? Eliza had a feeling she would never know the answer.

Two weeks after NaNoot returned home, she died at the age of eighty. She did not have a wrinkle in her face, and although her eyes were closed in the coffin, Eliza was certain they were still green and would remain so, forever. Joseph was at the funeral, whispering, "Sleep, my sister. Sleep." Eliza saw him touch NaNoot's blond hair. Her features were chiseled, like those of a white woman, and even her speech did not give away her black blood. But none of that mattered anymore. NaNoot was buried in the colored cemetery just outside of Lafayette.

CHAPTER FOURTEEN

THE JAPANESE MAGNOLIAS burst into February, painting the sky with purple and white blossoms. That was the first hint that spring had arrived, even though the mornings were still cold, with frost lacing the roofs of the buildings. The house was finally finished. Oscar made the carpenters correct all the mistakes and paid Dugas and his helpers in full. After the debris was cleaned up, Oscar sat on the front steps and studied the far end of the porch, trying to decide if it was the angle of the light which made the floor look wider at one end. He remembered his conversation with Robert Cormier, when they discussed the questionable skill of Claude Dugas. Oscar got out his ruler and measured the porch floor. "I cannot believe Dugas made the same mistake here," he said out loud. "The porch is wider on this end." Walking through the house he looked for the corner in the dining room which he had asked the unsupervised helpers to square off. Looking up at the ceiling he saw a gap about three inches wide in that corner.

"Oscar, where are you?" Eliza called out.

"I'm here," he answered pointing to the ceiling. "Look at that corner, it's terrible!"

Eliza looked around the dining room. "That is not a big thing," she said. "Look how beautiful the sun looks on the floors. They shine like mirrors." The hallway was bathed in rainbows from the glass in the front door, and Eliza sighed. "There is no other house like this one."

"Well, Cher," Oscar said, "that is true, in more ways than one! What are we going to do with this?" He pointed to a jog in the wall next to the front door.

144

"I saw that," Eliza said. "I've already decided what to do. I think a piano would fit just right in that strange little space."

He looked at Eliza. "What piano?"

"The one I will get for Christmas," she replied.

"Mama? Mama?" The little voice came from the porch.

"Millie, is that you?" Oscar called down the hall. Long ago he decided to call Mildred by the name Millie, and it didn't take long for everyone in the family to use the new name.

"Yes, Papa," Millie answered, pushing the front door open. "Souri says for Mama to come and rock Lloyd because he won't stop crying."

"Why don't you try rocking him?" Oscar said.

Millie looked up at her father. "No sir, not me. He'll just cry louder if I rock him. Besides, Theresa says Mama will have to rock him forever."

Eliza rubbed her husband's arm. "Lloyd is probably my last baby. You can't blame me for spoiling him a little bit."

"I understand, Cher, but you may be hurting him in the long run. Suppose something happens to you, then what?"

"Nothing is going to happen to me. Besides, Lloyd really does not cry all that much anyway."

"When are we going to live here for real?" Millie asked, looking down the hall.

Oscar laughed. "When would you like to move in?"

"Tomorrow, Papa!"

"We will have Christmas in the new house. How does that sound?

Throughout that summer the grown children often drove in to see the new house. Oscar received a lot of advice and very little help in deciding where to plant the orange tree brought from Eagle

145

Crest, and how wide to make the fence rails for the horse pasture. Anna told Oscar he should plant the bridal wreath to the left of the side door and Eliza told him it would not get enough sun on the left.

When Jules saw the house he was amazed. "You have done a good job, Papa," he said. "I'm certain the carpenters gave you trouble. I heard stories about that, but this is a beauty. You and Mama deserve every bit of it!"

Jules saved some of his money which he offered to Eliza for the house. She refused, saying he should keep it for something he needed in the seminary. "But Mama," he argued, "I am going to study in Rome. I will be gone for three years at least, and it will be difficult to send you money."

Although Eliza knew he wanted to study in Rome, his announcement caught her by surprise. "When will you leave?"

"In January," he replied. "I'll be here for Christmas, so please accept this as a present from me."

Eliza had tears in her eyes. "Will you be ordained in Rome?"

"Yes," he answered. "That is the plan."

"What an honor," she said shaking her head. "I am so blessed that God has given you to me." She placed her hands over his as he handed her the money. "I have had so many dreams for all of my children," she said, "but you, Jules have fulfilled them all."

On moving day, Joseph and Jefferson arrived in two wagons full of furniture and clothes and managed to unload everything before dark. Oscar was amazed that Eliza knew beforehand where to put it all. How do women do that? he wondered. Eliza decided that George would sleep upstairs alone, "until Lloyd is old enough to join him," she said. The only room lacking furniture was the parlor. Whenever the children passed the door of the empty room they cried out, "Mama, when are we going to get some furniture in here."

Anna was perhaps the most inconvenienced by the lack of someplace to sit because during her visits she often entertained her boyfriends. She improvised by pulling chairs away from the dining room table and positioning them in a semi circle in front of the fireplace. "I suppose this will have to do for tonight," she told Millie and Lydia who were always watching with great interest. When Anna drove in one Friday afternoon, followed by Allen Darby's furniture truck, no one was really surprised. She told the delivery men to set the bronze velvet sofa near the fireplace, with its side toward the bay windows. There were two matching chairs and an ottoman which were placed opposite the sofa. A new rocker for Eliza was placed in the curve of the bay, bathed in sunshine from the three windows overlooking College Avenue.

"This living room set is Mama's Christmas present," Anna told her brothers and sisters.

"Yeah, right!" Lucille said. "Bet you have someone in mind to help you keep that sofa warm."

"And we know who that is," Millie whispered to Lydia. The two girls disappeared down the hall and into the bedroom which had a fireplace back to back with the fireplace in the parlor. Millie put her eye up to a small space which ran along one side of the fireplace.

"Perfect!" she whispered. "Come and look."

Lydia stood on her tip toes and peeked through the crack. "Oh, I can see Anna sitting on the sofa."

"Good," Millie said, taking a deep breath. "Now all we have to do is wait until her boyfriend comes over."

As Millie predicted, the next Saturday night there was a knock on the front door which sent Anna flying down the hall. "Hello James," she said. "Please come in." Anna walked with her boyfriend to the parlor. The two of them sat on the new sofa, and before long James placed his arm around Anna's shoulders. In the bedroom behind the parlor, Millie and Lydia looked through the small space next to the fireplace.

"Look at that!" Millie whispered. "He has his arm around her!" Lydia giggled.

"What was that?" James asked.

"I don't know," Anna replied. "It sounded like a squeak, don't you think?"

"It can't be a mouse," he said as he walked up to the fireplace.

Anna stood up. "I know what that was!" She walked down the hall and into the bedroom where she was shocked to find her two little sisters with their noses pressed against the fireplace wall.

"What are the two of you doing?" Anna asked.

Millie jumped back. "Looking at a little mouse," she said.

"That's enough!" Anna cried out, and pulling the girls away from the wall, she put her eye up to the crack. "I cannot believe you would spy on me. How long have you been looking through that hole?"

When Eliza walked into the room, the children fell silent. "What are all of you doing here?" she asked, looking steadily at Millie and Lydia. "If it is what I think it is, then both of you should go into the other bedroom and wait until I can talk to you alone."

Everyone thought the spying issue had been settled until one day Millie made the comment to Theresa that looking through the crack was really boring since no one ever did anything anymore.

Christmas in the New House

As the schools closed for the holidays, the Daigle children arrived at the new house one by one. Eliza expected to see Anna and Idea right away because they were the closest, but when Cady arrived from the convent, after an absence of five years, Eliza was overwhelmed.

"Cady, I cannot believe you are finally here! Let me look at you! What a wonderful Christmas present to have you back!"

Oscar heard his daughter's name and walked into the hall. In her nun's habit, Cady seemed to be cut out of a piece of black and white paper. Only her eyes looked familiar. Speechless, he watched as she walked up to him.

"Papa," she said, tears filling her green eyes. "It's me, Papa. It's Cady." She hugged him tightly, and then pulled back. "Did you miss me?" she asked.

"Yes," he said, his lips quivering.

Cady looked at her father's face, reading all the pain that was there. "It's OK to hug me, Papa,"

"But I've never hugged a nun before."

"I was your daughter before I was a nun," she replied.

It was Eliza's rule that two days before Christmas Eve Oscar and Joseph were to choose which tree on the plantation would fall. The area behind the old house was filled with oak trees, and an occasional cedar and pine, as well. Eliza preferred the pine for a Christmas tree because the limbs were stiff enough to hold the ornaments. That year George and Armand cut down a long leaf pine and loaded it onto the wagon which was hitched to two horses.

"Mama will not like this one," George said. "It's at least twelve feet long. That's too big. We'll have to cut the top off just to get it through the door of the new house."

Armand shook his head. "The proper way to make a tree fit into a room is to cut it from the bottom."

"What do you mean?" George replied. "Did you learn that while you were studying to be a teacher?"

There was a long silence while George and Armand steadied the tree in the wagon. Armand smiled at his little brother. "I guess that was just common sense," George said. "They don't teach that in school, do they?"

As the wagon pulled up to the porch of the new house, the family cheered. Once the tree was decorated, Anna placed several presents under the tree. "They're not fancy," she told Eliza, "but I gave each gift a lot of thought."

Presents continued to appear under the tree as each of the children brought something to give, but none matched the present which Idea Landry gave to Eliza on Christmas Eve. When Idea and Pierre arrived in a wagon carrying a large object wrapped in blankets, everyone ran to meet them.

"Grandma!" Lucille called out. "What is that? Is it a present?"

"Yes, darlings, it is," she answered. "Go and find your brothers so they can help."

Eliza was in the kitchen when Lucille and Hilda burst through the doorway. "Mama, come quickly, and bring all the men," Hilda cried out. "Grandma is here with the biggest present of all!"

When Idea pulled away the blankets, Eliza saw the piano, and her eyes filled with tears. "Oh, Mama," she said. "How did you know?"

"I asked the children what I could give to you for Christmas," Idea answered. "Millie was the only one who had any suggestions. She said you wanted a piano for Christmas and you would put it in that funny little nook by the front door." Although the jog in the wall of the hallway was a mistake made by the carpenters, the piano looked beautiful there, bathed in the light from the windows.

"Merry Christmas, Eliza," Idea said. "Now you must learn to play it."

On that Christmas Eve the night sky was filled with stars. The children gathered on the front porch with Oscar and Eliza, and told stories about all the times they waited up for Santa, even though they knew for certain he would only come once they went to sleep.

"Papa," Millie whispered, "is there really a Santa Clause?"

Oscar took a big puff on his pipe, making it glow in the darkness. "Why do you ask that question, Millie?"

"I know he brings me presents, Papa, but I've never seen him," she replied.

"Do you believe that you have a guardian angel," Oscar asked.

"Yes," Millie said.

"Have you ever seen your guardian angel?"

"No," she answered.

"Well, Santa is like your guardian angel," Oscar said. "You never see him, but he is there, just as surely as we are all sitting here, together. Do you understand?"

Millie looked at her father in the dim light of the street lamp. "Yes, Papa," Millie replied. "I understand."

After the younger children were presumably in bed, Eliza brought out some of the presents which were to be the ones from

Santa Clause. Oscar picked up a small red horn and could not resist putting it up to his lips and blowing softly.

Millie heard the sound of the horn and crept into the middle bedroom. She quickly found the crack which ran alongside the fireplace and once served as a peephole for her spying, and through that hole she saw Oscar with the horn in his hand. Millie caught her breath and quickly ran back to her bedroom. As she lay there, her heart raced as she tried to pretend nothing had happened. After a while she realized she saw only the horn in her father's hand, and decided it would be just as he said. "Santa is like my guardian angel," she whispered. "He will come later."

CHAPTER FIFTEEN

THE START OF school after the holidays was always a letdown. The fun was officially over, and all that remained were hours of homework and piles of books all the way to Easter. After-school snacks were a grand event then. The aroma of baked sweet potatoes and hot bread greeted the children as they walked up the steps of the front porch.

"Just smell that," George cried out as he threw back his head to catch the full effects of Eliza's treats.

"I hope Mama still has some sweet pickle relish," Millie sighed. "That's my favorite to put on sweet potatoes!"

"Hurry up everyone," Lucille cried out as she walked up behind her brothers and sisters who by now had burst into the hallway and were running towards the kitchen. "I smell Mama's fresh coffee."

Oscar brought Eliza fresh figs and peaches from Eagle Crest and she canned them in syrup so thick the children used a knife to spread the preserves across slices of hot bread. Other times she stuffed the preserves into sweet dough pies and gave one to each child to dip into a cup of warm milk. As the children ate, Eliza asked questions about school and always listened to their answers with a great deal of interest.

Once George asked her, "Don't you ever get tired of listening to us?"

"No, I don't," she replied. "I never went to school like you do. I was taught at home by a tutor. When you tell me what you have done and what you have learned, I can imagine myself there with you. It makes me happy."

When that school year ended, everyone decided to stay in the city for the summer, and for the first time no one but Oscar went to the plantation. He still asked Eliza to go with him to the old house, but she had acquired a large circle of friends who paid regular visits to her at the house on College Avenue.

Lesson in Love

"Oh, but my dear Eliza," laughed Madeline Gilbert. "Surely you don't believe everything you hear!"

Eliza held her coffee cup tightly with both hands and looked steadily at her cousin Genevieve Landry. "I am only repeating what was told to me by Father Richard," she replied. "Of course, he is retired now, and perhaps does not know the whole story."

Madeline pursed her lips and eyed Eliza. "Don't you think a girl's family doctor would be the first to know? My husband told me he was never consulted by the girl's parents; therefore it is bound to be just a rumor."

"Doctor's don't always know everything, Madeline," Genevieve said, breaking her silence. "A prominent young girl who is suddenly sent away to help care for a sick aunt in Baton Rouge is a likely story, don't you agree?"

"No, I don't," Madeline replied. "I don't agree at all. I happen to know the aunt who is sick, and that is exactly where this girl is. I can't imagine how the rumor got started that she is pregnant!"

"Look Madeline," Genevieve said, "my cousin does not make up stories, and neither does Father Richard. Eliza, tell Madeline the story again."

154

Madeline turned to Eliza and smiled. "Yes, dear. Please do tell me again. Perhaps there was some part I missed."

Eliza shook her head and took a deep breath. "The only reason I got involved in this is because Father Richard asked for my help," she answered. "The mother of the girl suggested to him that I might ask either Anna or Ida to take her daughter in until she has her baby."

The conversation was interrupted by the noise of the front door slamming as Oscar walked down the hall and suddenly appeared in the parlor.

"Ladies," he nodded. "Eliza, may I see you alone for a moment?"

Madeline and Genevieve exchanged glances as Eliza quickly left the room. "Oscar, what is wrong?" she whispered.

"Have you talked to Souri today?" he asked.

"No. Why? What has happened?"

"Souri's mother is very ill. Joseph will need your help."

"Oh, no!" Eliza said. "Why didn't Souri tell me today?"

Oscar looked at his wife. "Because she did not want to bother you and your friends. I know you enjoy their company, perhaps a little too much. You need to attend to your family and servants. They need you more than these two gossiping women."

Oscar walked into their bedroom and shut the door, leaving Eliza to stare blankly at the vacant spot he left in the hallway. *I've never seen him do this before,* she thought. *What could be wrong?*

She returned to the parlor and excused herself, saying that she would have to tend to Isabel. As Eliza watched her friends leave, she felt a strange sensation in the pit of her stomach. "There is more to Oscar's reaction than Isabel's illness," she said aloud.

The trip to Eagle Crest was made at dusk, and Eliza had forgotten what it was like to ride through the countryside as the setting sun laced the horse and surrey with gold. She could smell springtime, and in the dim light, she saw the row of workers' houses strung out like grey pearls in the distance. As she and Oscar pulled the surrey up to Joseph's little house, Jefferson and his father met them with lanterns.

"I'm glad to see you, Miss Eliza," Joseph said as he helped her out of the surrey. "Isabel is doing poorly and talks about you. Souri is scared, and so are we."

Eliza walked into the house. It had been a long time since she had been there. Leocade's sewing machine was still in the corner, and through the doorway she could see some of the old pictures hanging on the kitchen wall. A small lantern flickered on a table in the corner of the room where Isabel lay in bed. Eliza touched her hand and she opened her eyes and smiled.

"Why, Miss Eliza," she whispered, "what are you doing here?"

"I've come to take care of you, Isabel," Eliza replied.

"No, child," Isabel said, "the good Lord and his son Jesus are right here. They will take care of me."

Eliza studied Isabel's face. Her skin had faded from black to a soft grey, the color of the wood on the workers' houses. Her once sparkling eyes were sunken and lifeless beneath a cloud of snow white hair.

"I will stay until you are well," Eliza answered.

Isabel closed her eyes and her dry lips parted in a smile. Eliza touched her cold hands and pulled the blanket up around Isabel's shoulders. Joseph sat at the foot of the bed and buried his face in a towel. His broad shoulders had withered away, and all that was left of his thick hair was a small grey fringe which circled his bald head. Jefferson looked as though he had absorbed his father's muscles and the shirt he wore wrinkled across his chest as he leaned against the door frame.

"Doc says it's her heart," Jefferson whispered.

"Where is Souri and where are your sisters and Lucius?" Eliza asked.

"Souri is in the kitchen," Jefferson answered. "She's pretty broke up about all this. My two other sisters are asleep and no one has seen Lucius since last summer."

When Eliza walked into the kitchen she found Souri sitting alone in the darkness, her cheeks wet with tears. Souri began to cry as Eliza wrapped both arms around her and held her close.

"Oh, Miss Eliza, thank goodness you've come," she said.

"Don't tell her good-by yet," Eliza said. "Come and sit down next to me. When did she get sick?"

Souri wiped her eyes with her sleeve and looked at Eliza. "Last week Momma had a dream. She said she talked to my little brother who died. She said he wanted her to come and get him and bring him home."

"Was Isabel sick then?" Eliza asked.

"I don't think so, Miss Eliza," Souri answered. "She did all her work, just like normal. But two days ago, she began to breathe real hard, like she had been running, or something. And then she got real tired and went to bed, and that's where she's been ever since."

"Is she eating and drinking?"

"Not a bite. Not a drop. She says she doesn't want anything."

Eliza took Souri's hands in hers. "Perhaps she just needs to rest. Don't you want to sit with her so that she knows you are near?"

"You don't understand, Miss Eliza," Souri cried out. "She wanted me to leave here. She said I should go away and not

157

become like her. She said she was nothing else but hired help. She said we were all no better than slaves."

Eliza shook her head. "No, that's not true. You and your family have become part of our family, and we have loved all of you."

"I know that, Miss Eliza, and I told her that. And I said that she should leave and go to the city and find good work, like NaNoot. Momma could have been something else but a cook and a cleaning woman."

"But she stayed," Eliza said. "There must have been a reason."

"She was too old and too tired to go anywhere," Souri sobbed. "Besides, when I told her I was happy and didn't want to leave, she said that was the problem. People like us don't know how to leave."

~ ~ ~ ~

At the funeral, the minister said there was nothing wrong with Isabel's heart. "It was a good one, strong and full of courage," he said. "God decided to let Isabel rest after all these years of taking care of her family and the plantation."

"Amen!" the congregation called out. "Amen!"

"And my brothers and sisters," the minister continued, "she is happy now. She is restored to health. She is with her little boy and her parents and grandparents. She is with the Savior, Jesus, and the Father."

"Amen!" the congregation called out again. "Praise the Lord."

Clearing his throat, the minister looked at Souri. "You told me Isabel said our kind of people don't know how to leave. Is that right?"

Souri nodded.

"Well, Souri, yesterday your mother left this earth in a white chariot, drawn by glorious angels and surrounded by all the generations of people who went before her. She left behind the people she loved the most, but God needed her and He taught her how to leave so that she could join Him in heaven."

Oscar and Edward helped Joseph and Jefferson carry the wooden coffin down to the spot under the old oak where Jefferson's son William was buried. All of the men workers had taken turns digging the hole for Isabel, and now they took turns filling it up, humming and singing as they passed the shovel from one to the other. Eliza listened to them, and remembered hearing that sound at night from the fields as the workers picked cotton by the light of a full moon. For the first time in her life, she realized a part of her had changed and now she understood why her mother taught her to be afraid of the workers. Her mother knew Eliza would love the people who loved her, even though her skin was white, and a piece of her heart would remain forever with these people and Eagle Crest.

Souri returned to the city house just a few days after the funeral. When Eliza suggested she take more time to mourn, Souri said her heart was broken, and couldn't break anymore. Not long after Isabel died Joseph saw Lucius standing under the old oak, looking down at his mother's name carved in the stone.

"Where have you been, son?" Joseph asked.

"I hitchhiked to Baton Rouge, Papa," Lucius sobbed. "I thought I could get a job over there. NaNoot told me about Mama as soon as I got back to her house. I guess I stayed gone too long."

CHAPTER SIXTEEN

WHEN HILDA WAS fourteen, she told Eliza she would enter the convent on her sixteenth birthday, and to Eliza's surprise, Theresa said she would like to become a nun also. Oscar was told of the intentions of his two daughters, and he was not surprised. He just sighed and said, "I know there is nothing I can do about this, so I will say nothing about it!"

Eliza was not so quick to agree, at least where Hilda was concerned. She had always thought Hilda was one of the prettiest of the children, and although she never voiced her opinion, as Hilda grew many people confirmed what Eliza thought. One of the people was Bishop Frances who actually told Hilda, "A woman who looks like you should not enter the convent."

During many conversations with Hilda, Eliza attempted to persuade her to reconsider. "What will Rose do?" Eliza asked her. "She is so attached to you?"

"But Mama," Hilda replied, "I feel that God is calling me to teach, and I want to be like the sisters at The Convent."

"Have you talked to Cady about this?"

"Yes, I have," Hilda answered. "Cady told me a lot of things, but it really doesn't matter how she feels about being a nun, it is something I want to do."

"You know, of course, that Theresa will probably follow you," Eliza said.

"Yes, I do. If that is what she wants then she should be allowed to become a nun also."

160

The same day that Hilda entered the novitiate, Eliza received a letter from Gabriel announcing that he had married a girl from Oklahoma. "I'll bring her to meet you soon, Mama," he wrote. "Kiss everyone for me and tell them I miss them." Eliza knew nothing about Oklahoma, but she had heard from Madeline that a lot of Indians lived there. When Oscar asked Eliza how she felt about Gabriel's news she replied, "I suppose the marriage is alright, but don't like him living in Oklahoma with all those Indians."

Oscar laughed. "What makes you think Indians are bad?"

"I've been told by people who know that Indians are savages," she replied.

The subject of Gabriel and his bride was dropped until Oscar saw Eliza poring over a map of the United States. "What are you looking for, Cher?" he asked.

"I'm looking for Oklahoma," she replied. "Come and show me where it is!"

"Here," Oscar said as he placed his finger on the state. "See the one with the Indian head on it?"

"Are there really many Indians there?"

"I've heard there are," Oscar said, "but there are a lot of Indians around here also. You know, I have Indian blood in me and that means your children do also."

"What!" Eliza gasped. "How do you know that?"

Oscar sat down beside his wife and told her the story his mother told him when he was a little boy. "Etienne Daigle left Canada and traveled to Louisiana where he made his home. In those days, ships from France sailed to New Orleans filled with things the people living here couldn't buy in any stores. Etienne Daigle made a living bringing those things by ship to the French

161

and the Acadians living in St. Louis. He traveled by boat up the Mississippi River, and during one of his trips, he met an Indian girl named Marie. At first he didn't know that she was royalty. When he asked her to marry him and come here to Louisiana he discovered he was in love with an Indian princess."

"No!" Eliza said. "You are making that story up! No one in your family looks like an Indian princess!"

"How do you know?" Oscar laughed. "Most of us have blue eyes, and she had blue eyes, and fair skin. Besides, didn't you ever wonder why I never worried about the crops during a dry spell?"

"I never noticed," Eliza replied.

"Well, I never did worry. Want to know why?"

"Not really," she said, looking at the map again.

"Sure you do," Oscar laughed. "It's because I knew I could dance and make it rain anytime I wanted to!"

Oscar ducked in time to avoid getting hit with an oversized sofa pillow. "I can't stand you when you make fun of my questions," Eliza whispered between clinched teeth. "None of that was true, right?"

"On the contrary, Cher," he answered. "All of it is true."

CHAPTER SEVENTEEN

ELIZA WAS WORRIED about her mother. During Idea's visit, she told Eliza she was having trouble sleeping. Eliza knew it was more than that because her mother looked pale and seemed weak and unsteady.

Perhaps she is worried about something, Eliza thought. She decided to wait until her mother and Pierre were back in Côte Gelée, then she would call. The hours crawled by. Eliza looked at the clock and then picked up the phone. After several rings she heard her mother's voice.

"Hello? Eliza? Did I forget something?"

"No, Mama," Eliza answered, "I am worried about you. It's obvious you are not feeling well."

"I'm just getting old, I think," Idea replied. "I can't do the things I used to do. If I feel really sick I'll call you."

Eliza hung up. She had an uneasy feeling in the pit of her stomach. "I'm worried about Mama," she told Oscar that evening.

"Why don't you call one of your sisters and ask if they have noticed anything?" he said.

Eliza knew it was too late now, but tomorrow, she thought, I'll call Helen. That night, in the quiet darkness, she shut her eyes and saw her family around the dinner table. Her mother was at one end, her father at the other, and sitting with them, Alcide and Pierre, then Edmond and Emelie. Across the table were Helen, Marie and Julie. With her eyes still shut, Eliza saw the clock on her mother's mantel the morning Emelie died. Its hands were stopped at four o'clock.

"Wake up, Cher," Oscar whispered as he shook Eliza gently. "You are having a bad dream."

She sat up in bed. "Oh, Oscar, I saw all of us around Mama's table. Papa was there, and so was Emelie. What does this mean?"

"Probably nothing," Oscar said as he rubbed her back. "Lie down, and go back to sleep."

When morning came Eliza felt as though she had not slept at all. She heard the sounds of the children playing in the hallway, and Souri's voice calling Lloyd from the kitchen. Looking out of the window, she saw heavy rain clouds catching the sunlight and squeezing it into long yellow ribbons across the rooftops and trees.

"Lord, child," Souri sang out, "you know better than to bring that dog into this house! Now go wash your hands!"

Lloyd saw Eliza and began to cry. "Mama, Souri's being mean."

Eliza watched as Souri tied a rope around the little dog's neck and led her out the back door. "Souri is doing what I told her to do, Lloyd. Now stop crying and go wash your hands."

"Oh, Miss Eliza, I don't take to animals in the house," Souri said.

"Neither do I," Eliza replied. "Souri, there is something I want to ask you. I don't think Mama looks well. Have you noticed that?"

"Yes, Miss Eliza, I have," Souri replied. "She seems kinda pale to me, and yesterday, as she was leaving I saw her grab hold of the doorway, like she was gonna fall."

Eliza shook her head. "I'd like for her to see a doctor, but she says she is just getting old."

"Well, Miss Eliza, that's how these old people are! They tell you they gonna be all right, and the next thing you know, they're dead."

Eliza never could remember her sister Helen's telephone number and she didn't want to call Julie because she was afraid her mother would answer. Marie was probably teaching. Eliza tapped on the phone's lever and Miss Grace answered, "Number please?"

"Hello? This is Eliza Landry, I mean Daigle now. I would like for you to ring my sister Helen for me."

There was a short silence, then a short ring and Helen answered. "Eliza, I was going to call you. Pierre just called me. Mama is too weak to get out of bed. I am going there now. Perhaps you should come also."

"Yes, I will, certainly. Yes," Eliza stammered. "Souri, come here. Quickly! Saddle Crescent," Eliza said, fighting back the tears. "Mama's sick and I've got to go."

Souri placed her hand on Eliza's arm. "But you haven't ridden in years, and I think it's gonna rain, Miss Eliza. Wait until Mr. Oscar comes back with the surrey. He'll go too!"

"No, no, no!" Eliza replied. "He's at the plantation. No telling how long he'll be there. It's harvest time. Souri, No! Do as I say."

Eliza stared at the inside of her satchel. It looked as though it could hold a day's worth of clothes, and she could hang it from the saddle if she had to. She packed quickly, watching the gathering storm clouds through the window. The last thing Eliza put into the satchel was the Bible her mother had given her. The ribbon was still marking Idea's favorite passage. "The Lord is my shepherd," Eliza said aloud, "I shall not want."

Souri led Crescent to the front of the house and heard Eliza's sobs. "Oh, Miss Eliza, please stay here. Your Mama's going to be all right. Don't go getting yourself sick or hurt. Wait until Mr. Oscar comes back!"

Eliza put her foot in the stirrup and pulled herself into the saddle. "Souri, get something ready for the children to eat when they come home from school. Tell Oscar I will call him tonight." As she pulled the reins, Eliza was surprised to see Crescent turn slowly and begin to walk through the front yard toward College Avenue. The horse would have continued if Jules had not driven up. Running up to his mother, he put his arms up and embraced her as she climbed down from the horse.

"Oh, Jules," Eliza sobbed, "you are like an angel, here whenever I need you."

Jules held his mother's face in his hands. "Mama, what is wrong? Where are you going?"

"Your grandmother is very sick, and I need to go to her," Eliza answered. "Your father has gone to the plantation for the harvest."

"Give me your things," Jules said, "and bring Crescent back to Souri. I'll take you, Mama."

This was Eliza's first ride in an automobile, and she sat in awe as the scenery flew by, like pieces of colored paper in the wind. She held on to the edge of the seat and stared through the windshield.

"Do you always drive this fast?" she asked her son.

Jules laughed. "Crescent actually runs faster than this," he said.

"How long have you been back from Rome?"

"Four days," Jules answered. "I have been with the bishop, and now I will be able to spend a few days here, with you, before I am assigned to a church parish."

Eliza had taken her eyes off the road and was looking steadily at her son. "I have seen pictures of the Pope. Does he look like his pictures?"

"Somewhat," Jules said, "but in person, his holiness and humility are what you see. He is not an ordinary man."

166

Souri's prediction of rain came true and large drops began to hammer the roof of the automobile. "What's that?" Eliza whispered.

"It's raining," Jules whispered back.

The discussion turned to the advantages of an automobile over a horse. Jules listed shelter from the elements as one, but as the rain continued, the road turned to mud and made driving almost impossible.

When it became obvious to Eliza that they might get stuck, she said, "Well, son, a horse would not have let a little mud stop him, and we would be at Grandma's house by now!"

"Has Papa ever talked about getting an automobile?" Jules asked.

Eliza smiled. "He has driven one only once, and he kept yelling 'Whoa' instead of putting his foot on the brake. The owner of the car was your father's friend, and he said he would bring the automobile back when your father learned how to drive."

Jules and Eliza saw several automobiles parked in front of Idea's house, one of which was Dr. Gilbert's. Alcide and Pierre were waiting on the front porch.

"Helen told us you would be coming," Alcide said, "but she didn't tell us Jules would be with you."

"I surprised her," Jules answered, "and had to pull her off her horse. She didn't want to wait for Papa."

"How's Mama?" Eliza asked.

Alcide shook his head. "Let's go inside."

"Eliza," Dr. Gilbert said, "we've been waiting for you, but this is a surprise to see Jules! As I was saying," he continued, "Idea appears to have pneumonia. We have seen a lot of that lately, probably a result of the flu. That illness always hits the elderly hard, and she has had a high fever for several days now, although she never told anyone apparently." Gilbert looked carefully at each one of the children. "I don't want to give you false hope. She may recover, only time will tell, but her age is against her. Typically, pneumonia will ravage the body for seven days, then a crisis is reached, the fever breaks, and the body overcomes the illness."

"What can we do?" Eliza asked.

"You can pray," he answered. "You should all remain here, close by, for the next week. We will count today as the first day of the seven, and God willing, she will get well."

Idea lay in bed with her left hand across her chest, her wedding ring reflecting the soft light which seemed to surround her.

"Mama," Eliza whispered.

Idea opened her eyes. "Eliza, my darling, how did you know?"

"I knew, Mama. I just knew. I'm here now. Go back to sleep."

Eliza could hear Julie crying softly. "Mama is in God's hands," Eliza said. "When you feel frightened, pray Julie. That's all we can do."

After it was all over, Eliza looked back on that week as though it was a dream. The days and nights were filled with fears, and sometimes smiles when Idea would eat a little food or drink a few swallows of water. The fever seemed worse at night and Eliza piled blankets on Idea to stop her shivering. Her breathing was so shallow that the children were afraid to leave her. As the days drifted by, Idea began to slip away. She slept longer and seemed to be struggling to breathe.

Eliza often begged God, "Take the pneumonia away from Mama and give it to me!"

As Idea's children kept their watch around her bed they held their mother's hands and brushed their own tears from her pillow. Father Richard touched her eyes and her forehead with holy oil and asked the children to recite the "Our Father" as he whispered his Latin prayers for the sick. "Talk to her," he told them. "Tell her that you love her. She will hear you. Send her to God."

Eliza touched her mother's forehead. "Mama, it's me, Eliza. It's going to be all right, Mama." She kissed her mother and saw a tear roll down her cheek. Eliza caught the tear with her own tear soaked handkerchief and then pressed the piece of cloth against her lips. In that moment, Idea struggled to catch her breath, and then without a sound, she died.

~ ~ ~ ~

"But Papa," Millie cried, "Lydia and I want to go with you to the funeral!"

Oscar placed his hands on Millie's shoulders. "There is no more room in the surrey. We are bringing Lucille, and George and Jefferson plus two of the workers because they can help with the burial, and we will bring Julie back with us. She is going to live with us for awhile."

"What about Jules?"

"After the funeral, he will stay and try to do what he can to comfort everyone. I'm sorry, Millie, but you must understand. You cannot come. You must stay here and help Souri."

Millie and Lydia watched as Oscar hitched the horse to the surrey. "Well, it's just you and me, kid," Millie said, looking at Lydia and shrugging her shoulders.

"What about Rose and Florence, and Lloyd?" Lydia asked.

"They probably don't care, like we do," Millie replied, looking around and then motioning to Lydia. "Come here. I have an idea.

Let's ask Mr. Smith if he has room. Papa always said he was a good neighbor to have!"

Millie and Lydia stood on the Smith's front porch. "Looks like they have already left," Millie said as she knocked on the front door. To her surprise the door opened, and Mr. Smith stood there smiling at the two of them.

"Why, hello," he said. "How are you two young ladies doing today?"

Millie took a deep breath. "Fine, thank you. We need a big favor, Mr. Smith. Do you have room to take us with you to my Grandma's funeral?"

Harold Smith rubbed his chin and then cleared his throat. "Well, my dears, I don't think I will be going to your grandma's funeral because, you see, Mrs. Smith is not feeling well."

"Can't you go without her and take us instead," Lydia asked. "We don't take up much room."

"No, I'm certain you don't! But I can't leave Mrs. Smith. She might need me."

"For what?" Lydia asked again.

"She might need me to get her a cracker or a glass of water," he replied.

"Does she have a fever?" Lydia whispered. "Cause if she does then she might have what my grandma had, and my grandma died."

Millie looked at Lydia. "Mr. Smith already knows that. That's why there's a funeral."

That night, Souri asked where they had been and Millie replied "visiting" and kicked Lydia under the table. "Hush," she whispered. The two of them lay awake talking in the yellow circle made by the street light on their sheets.

"What does a dead person look like, Millie?" Lydia asked. Staring at the ceiling, Millie tried to remember all the things she had been told about death. "Dead people are all white, and cold and hard like a rock. Their eyes are shut, like they are asleep. But they really aren't asleep cause you can't wake them up for anything!"

"Where's Grandma now?"

"Right now? This minute?"

"Yes," Lydia sighed. "Right now!"

"Up in heaven, that's for sure," Millie replied, holding her hands up to make shadows on the wall next to the bed.

"Rose said Grandma is a ghost now and she's gonna come back and scare us if we're bad."

"Come back from heaven? Grandma? Naw, you don't have to worry about that," Millie said. "She's so happy up there! Why would she want to come back here to this old place and scare us? I mean, she loves us lots and probably wants us to be up there with her."

Lydia began to sob. "But I don't want to go to heaven. I don't want to die."

"Hush!" Millie whispered. "Someone is gonna come in here and think I'm beating you up."

Lydia buried her nose in her pillow. "I don't want Grandma to be a ghost."

"She's not a ghost, OK?"

"She's not?"

"No, definitely not a ghost!"

"What is she then?"

Millie looked at her little sister and smiled. "She's an angel."

The next day Eliza brought her sister, Julie, to Lafayette. "Stay with Oscar and me awhile," Eliza told her sister. "Mama would not

171

want you to be alone and there will be time enough for taking care of things. I'll take you back to Mama's house in a little while."

"I miss Mama," Julie said. "It all seems like a bad dream."

"I know," Eliza replied. "We were not ready for her to leave us."

"But she has not really left," Julie said. "She is right here with us. Don't you feel it?"

"Father Richard told me that when the parent dies, so does the child," Eliza answered. "I think that is why Mama's death is so hard for us. A part of us died with her."

Tante Julie

When Eliza's sister Julie arrived for a visit she was greeted with a cautious amount of friendliness and an equal amount of skepticism. She was not married and proudly said she never would be. She looked a great deal like Eliza, and in that respect she was pretty, with large brown eyes. However, she dressed only in black, wearing black hats when she went out and a black mantilla when she was at home.

"Why does she look like that?" Florence asked Eliza after watching Julie glide down the hallway.

"She likes to look that way," Eliza answered, trying hard not to laugh.

Slowly "Tante Julie" was accepted by the Daigle children. There remained, however, a certain mystique about her, and the children continued their speculations as to whether her legs went all the way down and did she wear roller skates for shoes.

That summer was unusually hot. There had been no rain for months and most of the crops had turned brown. From everything that he saw, Oscar was certain this harvest would be one of the worst. When he expressed his disappointment over the drought, Eliza told him, "Don't worry as long as you are able to harvest something for this year."

"But Cher, that's a lot of work wasted, and a lot of money lost," he replied.

"I know it is," she said, "but God must have other plans for you."

Oscar put his head in his hands. "He must want me to shrivel like a raisin in the hot sun!"

"I have an idea," Eliza said. "Why don't we take the whole family to White Lake for a swim and a picnic? It would be fun for all of us, especially Julie, since she told me she has never been swimming."

"Really?" Oscar said. "Why is that?"

"Probably because she was so much younger than everyone else, and the only girl left at home after Marie went into the convent. The boys swam, I'm sure, but they never thought about taking Julie."

Eliza had not been to the lake in several years. It had not changed much, although now it seemed bigger and more danger-ous. That day the water was filled with white caps and the shoreline was littered with branches and pine cones. They spread their blankets near a little beach where a giant cypress tree spread its exposed roots across a cliff, creating a cave in the sandy hillside. Oscar and Edward were already in the water with the boys by the time Eliza and the girls emerged in bathing suits and tested the water's edge with reluctant toes. The last to appear was Julie. She watched the waves for a moment, and then ran splashing into the water.

"Look at that!" George said. "She likes it!"

Eliza was uneasy. The wind was picking up, and she kept listening for thunder. "I think we need to eat our lunch now," she said. "We may get rain before tonight."

After lunch Oscar decided to pack up. Lightning began to cut through the clouds and claps of thunder sounded in the distance like giant bowling balls rolling across the sky.

"Well, at least we got some fun out of this," George said. "And, I must admit Tante Julie looks pretty good in a bathing suit."

Oscar grinned. "Yes, she does. In fact I think she looks like Joan Crawford. Don't you, Cher?"

The Daigle children accepted Julie after the trip to the lake. She was the first girl into the water, and that meant a great deal. She also taught them how to play the piano, bake cookies, and make peach and syrup sandwiches. Soon Julie and Lucille were like sisters, and it was Lucille who solved the mystery of the tin cans.

Each morning Julie walked around the house saying the rosary and each night she laid out her clothes for the next morning. First she chose which black dress to wear and then placed her black mantilla near it. After completing her outfit with black shoes and stockings, she turned out the light and always fell asleep quickly. One night Rose led Florence and Lydia into Julie's dark room, and without making a sound the three girls found the dress Julie planned to wear the next day and tied tin cans to the inside of the hem.

In the morning Lydia knocked on Julie's door. "Tante Julie, would you please make a peaches and syrup sandwich for me?"

"I suppose so," Julie answered. "Go and wait for me in the kitchen." As she emerged from the bedroom the tin cans made a scrapping noise against the hall floor. She stopped and looked

174

behind her. Julie continued down the hall, stopping again in the dining room to look behind her. She shook her skirt, then went into the kitchen.

"Lydia, here is your sandwich," Julie said. "Now sit quietly please while I say my rosary." Julie took a few steps and then stopped when the scrapping noise returned. She glared at Lydia. "What is that noise? Did you drop something, Lydia?"

"No, Ma'am," Lydia answered.

Julie stopped and looked down at the front hem of her dress. She took another step and the cans rattled again. Julie stopped and this time she grabbed the back of her dress and discovered the cans. "Lucille," she called out, "come here please!"

"What have they done to you, Julie?" Lucille gasped.

"I don't know," she replied, "tied cans to my dress, I guess. I don't know why they did this, or when."

Lucille put her finger up to her lips. "Shhhh," she whispered, and walking out into the hall she listened to the giggles coming from the bathroom. Flinging open the door she discovered Rose and Florence. "I cannot believe how you behave toward Julie," Lucille said. "You should all be ashamed of yourselves."

Just as she promised, Eliza took Julie back to Côte Gelée, and one month later she called Eliza with the news that she had purchased a house in the city and would be moving.

"Where is the house?" Eliza asked with surprise.

"Not far from the church and very close to you," Julie replied. "You will have to come visit often!"

"Oh, no," Florence said, "I hope no one knows she is related to us."

The Donation

On one of the walls of The Convent chapel there was a stone marker with the name, Senator Francois Daigle. Oscar's father had given some of the land to the nuns to build a larger school. For this reason the principal of the school at the time of the donation decided to allow any future Daigle children to attend the school for a reduced tuition. "After all," she often told people, "Senator Daigle had his own grandchildren in mind when he donated the land." Regina Daigle was one of the first boarders of the school, and the rest of the Daigle children began their school years as students in the classroom of Tante Marie, Eliza's sister who was also a teacher and a nun. It never occurred to Eliza that someone might object to the fact that the Daigle family did not pay full tuition, but the new principal, Mother Dejean felt the arrangement was unfair to the other students.

"Mama? Mama? Mama!" Millie called as she walked down the hall toward the kitchen.

"In here, Millie," Eliza answered. "What is wrong? You are all red from running. Did you get into trouble at school?"

"I'm not in trouble Mama," Millie quipped. "Mother Dejean is!"

"What are you talking about?"

"Well, I think you should sit down before I tell you because it will make you so mad you will want to punch her in the nose."

"That's okay, Millie, I can punch standing up."

"Lydia and I were leaving to come home, and Mother Dejean asked us to go to her office. She said there was something she wanted to talk to us about. So we went, and get ready for this

176

Mama, she told us we would have to mop and sweep floors because you only pay a little bit of money for us to go to school."

"What did you say?"

"I told her about Grandpa Daigle and she said she already knew that and she said we would have to mop and sweep anyway. And, she said we needed to start today!"

"Where are your sisters and your brother?" Eliza asked.

"They're at school, sweeping and mopping! I ran all the way home to tell you."

Eliza immediately called the school, but it was after hours and no one answered. "I want my children home from school now. Millie, you are the oldest. Go back to school and get your sisters and Lloyd."

"Yes, Ma'am, but what will I say to Mother Dejean?"

"Tell her I will visit her in the morning, but that all of you will not be at school tomorrow!"

Just as Millie was leaving Lydia and Florence appeared, pulling Lloyd along between them. After Eliza and Oscar heard everyone's story, they both decided something had to be done, because, as Oscar said, "No other principal of the school ever objected to the tuition arrangement."

"We are not talking about a lot of money here," Oscar said. "What is the tuition? Six dollars a month for each child? We pay two dollars a month for each child. I think that is plenty!"

"I agree," Eliza answered, "but apparently Mother Dejean does not think we pay enough. There is only one thing to do." The next morning, after giving Souri strict instructions to keep everyone home from school, Eliza and Oscar set out in the surrey for The Convent. The morning bell had just rung when they drove up and Mother Dejean was still in the front yard watching the students file into their classrooms.

"Why, Mr. and Mrs. Daigle," Mother Dejean said, extending her hand to Oscar. "How nice of you to come to visit."

"Thank you," Oscar replied. "We would like a word with you, if you have the time."

Mother Dejean frowned, and glancing at Eliza she asked, "Is something wrong?"

"We feel there has been a misunderstanding," Eliza answered.

Mother Dejean led Eliza and Oscar up the front steps to her office. "What is the problem?" she asked.

Oscar paced back and forth in front of the principal. "Yesterday, our children were made to mop and sweep the floors after school. They were told they must do the chores of the school's janitor because we do not pay full tuition for our children. Is that correct?"

Mother Dejean's eyes were wide. "Yes, that is correct."

"Have you ever given other children these chores to do?" Eliza asked, suddenly feeling the blood rush to her head.

"No," Mother Dejean answered.

"Why not?" Oscar shot back.

"Because all the other families pay full tuition," she replied.

"Have any of these other families ever donated enough money to build buildings and expand the school?"

"No, Mr. Daigle."

"That is exactly my point. My children are an exception, and you can be certain Senator Daigle was thinking about them when he made his donation."

Mother Dejean looked at both Eliza and Oscar, and then tightening her jaw, she said, "There is nothing I can do. I'm sorry."

"Well, there is something we can do," Oscar replied. "Let's go, Cher, we have to register the children before noon."

"Where are you taking them?" Mother Dejean cried out.

"To public school," Eliza answered. "We hope to have them there by tomorrow morning."

Mother Dejean put her hand on Eliza's shoulder. "Are you sure you want to do this?"

"Yes," Eliza said, "we don't want our children mopping and sweeping floors for the rest of their school years."

Eliza fought back the tears as she and Oscar rode the few short blocks to Center School and registered the children for classes the next day. "Now Mother Dejean has no tuition from us!" Eliza whispered as they turned the surrey toward home.

"Oh, Miss Eliza!" Souri said. "That phone has plum rung itself off the hook on the wall. The Convent called, and Father Richard called, and I think a lady told me to tell you the bishop himself wants to talk to you! Lord of mercy, what have you done?"

"We put the children in public school," Eliza said. "They will start tomorrow."

"Papa," Lucille called from the hallway. "The bishop wants to talk to you!"

When the conversation with the bishop ended, Oscar motioned for Eliza to go to their bedroom, where he shut the door. "The Convent will send for all the children tomorrow morning. They will be excused for today, and we will not be charged any tuition for the rest of the time they attend the school."

CHAPTER EIGHTEEN

WHEN THE STOCK market crashed in 1929, everyone immediately feared the worst. It was a different kind of fear, though, because most of the panic was up north, in the big cities filled with banks and expensive real estate. Down south, in small towns like Lafayette, people gathered in saloons and churches, in restaurants and hotel lobbies. They discussed the economy and what went wrong and promised to help one another no matter what.

"I don't trust anyone to tell us the truth," Oscar told Eliza.

"What does the depression mean for us?" she asked.

"I don't know, Cher," he answered, "but as far as I can tell the people who will suffer the most will be the rich. They will lose their money, their savings, their jobs. We'll feel it, I'm certain, but we won't be poor because we have our land and our houses."

Eliza looked at her husband carefully. "Jefferson told me that it's no use bringing the crops to market because the mills can't pay the farmers. He said there's no money. Is that true?"

Oscar shook his head. "We will get paid something; it won't be a lot, however. The best thing to do is to hold on to as much as we can so that we will have enough to eat. Some of it can be used as barter also, until times get better."

"Will you be able to pay the workers?"

"Probably not," Oscar replied, "but Cher, they really don't need money from me. They can live off the land and still sell the moss they pick out of the trees and the cloth they weave. They'll make it if they stay on the plantation."

"I cannot believe all of this," Eliza said. "It's very frightening. I don't think we can live in this world without money." Eliza sat back in her rocker, closed her eyes and fell asleep. From somewhere far away she heard Joseph's words to her when she was Oscar's bride and Eagle Crest was new.

"The land will take care of you, feed you and make clothes for you," he said. "It will give you money after it makes you work hard, just like a mama does. It will teach you how to live. And, when you die, the land will cover you up so that you can sleep."

At first, Eliza did not hear Madeline Gilbert calling from the front porch. "I declare, why is this door locked?" she called out. "Eliza! Can you hear me? Who locked this door?"

Souri ran down the hall. "Oh, please be quiet, Miss Eliza is asleep. You best come back when she is awake."

"Nonsense, girl! I need to talk to her!" Madeline brushed past Souri and shook Eliza's shoulder. "Wake up Eliza, I have to talk to you!"

"What's the matter?" Eliza whispered. "What's happened?"

"Everything's happened! Everything's changed, and not for the better!"

By now Eliza was wide awake. "Are you in some sort of trouble?" she asked her friend.

"We all are!" Madeline answered, pulling up a chair and sitting squarely in front of Eliza. "I never believed it would come to this. My husband, a doctor of all things, is not getting paid for his services."

"Why not!" Eliza asked.

"Because no one has any money. They are paying, if you can call it that, with pigs and chickens and vegetables. Who ever heard of such a thing?" By now Madeline Gilbert was sobbing. "I can't take a pig to the milliner's and buy a hat, now can I?"

Eliza tried not to smile. "Have you tried? It might work."

"Oh, Eliza, this is not funny. People will starve. Already there are lines at Mrs. Smith's soup kitchen. And there are lines of men at the courthouse, waiting for the government to give them jobs. Bankers and professors are waiting side by side with railroad workers. What am I going to do?"

"Nothing," Eliza answered. "There is nothing you can do about this, except of course, pray."

"I can't live on prayer. How will we eat?"

"I thought you told me Dr. Gilbert was getting pigs and chickens and vegetables. That's food, Madeline, unless of course you need the pigs for something else."

She took a deep breath. "Aren't you afraid, Eliza?"

"Yes," Eliza replied, "I am afraid Eagle Crest will not be able to take care of us. I am afraid the banks will shut down and the businesses will close, and we will lose everything."

Madeline held Eliza's hand. "Will you help us Eliza, even though Oscar hates me?"

"Oscar does not hate anyone," Eliza said. "Yes, we will help if we can."

The Great Depression deepened. At first there were just rumors, then one of the biggest banks in Lafayette closed. The city was officially broke, and employees were paid with scrip. Oscar and Eliza did not discuss the depression in front of the children, and to the outside world the Daigle household seemed pretty normal.

~ ~ ~ ~

During the weeks following his high school graduation, George worked with Oscar on the plantation. Although he often told his father he enjoyed supervising the workers, Oscar knew George would eventually try to find work in Lafayette. Not far from the new house there was a small sheet metal shop owned by a Spaniard who brought his family to Lafayette to try to earn a living. Because of his age and eagerness to work, George was hired immediately, and it was not long before he became friends with Martin, one of the owner's sons. One afternoon as Martin was looking out of the shop window, Millie walked by on her way home from school.

"Hey Martin, we need your help," George called out. "What's up with the window?"

"Come here," Martin said. "Who is that girl?"

"That's my sister," George said. "Why?"

"She's a honey," Martin said. "What's her name?"

"Millie," George answered. "Yeah, she's a knockout all right, but not too smart. What a shame. Oh well, you can't have it all!"

"Spoken like a true brother," Martin laughed. "Does she have a boyfriend?"

"I don't think so," George replied. "I think most of the boys around here belong to my sister Lucille!"

"Not me," Martin said.

Before long Martin was sitting with Millie on the front porch of the Daigle house. Eliza and Souri watched them from the curtained window. "Look at that," Eliza said, "he is so little. He looks like a hummingbird! We will have to fatten him up."

~ ~ ~ ~

Anna arrived one week before Mother's Day in her car filled with cans of paint and paint brushes. "Mama, where are you?" she called out, walking from room to room in the house. "Your Mama is out with the horses," Souri called back.

Anna saw Eliza standing next to the back pasture fence, running her hand along Crescent's soft brown mane. "Mama! Happy Mother's Day early!" Anna sang out as she walked up to meet Crescent who, by now, had seen Anna and moved along the railing toward her.

Eliza smiled. "This always amazes me. Crescent still remembers you."

"I have a surprise for you, Mama," Anna said. "The others are coming here early and we're going to paint the house for you."

Eliza stared at Anna. "I didn't realize it needed painting."

"Well maybe not so much on the outside, but we're going to paint everything, inside and out, and fix anything that needs fixing. We know Papa isn't too good about that."

Eliza watched in amazement as the house was transformed by the children. By late afternoon the entire house was finished and everyone gathered on the front porch in time to watch the sunset.

"This is really nice," Edward said. "Everyone's here and we're all well and happy. It reminds me of the times we spent with Mama and Papa a long time ago."

"Edward told Mama some good news this morning," Millie said. "Go ahead. Tell them Edward."

"I am now principal of the school," Edward said.

"There's more," Millie whispered. "He is also the first principal in the entire parish to hire a colored woman as a teacher."

George buried his head in his arms. "A woman? You hired a woman? And a colored woman at that! Who in the world made you do that?"

"No one made me do anything," Edward answered. "Jobs are very difficult to find now and I am tired of watching men getting hired over and over again in spite of the qualifications of the women who applied for the same jobs. Maybe it's because I was always very close to Mama and all of my sisters. It really has nothing to do with the color of a person's skin."

"Edward, there's more to your feelings than that," Regina said. "Growing up your best friend was William, Jefferson's son, and that friendship has influenced the way you feel about colored people."

"I think you are right," Edward replied. "I remember the long talks William and I had. He was self-taught and knew more about life than several white kids put together!"

"George," Eliza said, "what makes you feel that colored people and women are inferior? You surely didn't learn that from this family."

"It's obvious why I feel that way," George replied. "From what I know colored people don't like to work, and they don't work. And women? They are too emotional to run anything important."

Oscar smiled. "Think about all the workers on the plantation, son. They do more work in one year than you will ever do in a lifetime. And they're happy and content."

"They're slaves, Papa. What do you expect?"

"Slavery was abolished a long time ago," Oscar said. "These are free men and women we are talking about. And as far as women running the show, you don't know what you are talking about. Women have been doing that for years, and they are so good at it we men don't even know they're doing it!"

~ ~ ~ ~

When Eliza asked Millie what she wanted as a high school graduation gift, she replied, "Money to buy my favorite perfume!"

Eliza's words caught in her throat as she told Oscar what Millie wanted. "Don't worry," he replied. "I will give her a little."

The next morning Millie found an envelope on her plate. "Oh Papa," she squealed as she held up several dollar bills, "Thank you! This is the best day of my life!" Millie gave the money to Lloyd and asked him to go to the drugstore and buy a little bottle of Chanel #5 cologne. To her surprise he returned in a short amount of time, saying he had lost it all.

"What!" Millie cried out. "You lost all my money? I have no cologne and no money? Is that what you are saying?"

Lloyd nodded.

"I cannot believe I trusted you with all the money I have in the world and you go and lose it all!"

"Aw, come on Sis," Lloyd replied. "It's just money."

"Easy for you to say. You don't care about anyone except yourself!" Millie sobbed.

"Son," Oscar said, "how could you lose your sister's money after she trusted you?"

Lloyd laughed. "Come on everyone, it was just a joke. Here Millie, here's your cologne and your money that was left over. Happy graduation."

Oscar walked up to his son and grabbing him by the collar he led him into the parlor and closed the door. "Uh-oh," whispered Souri, "he's gonna get it now."

~ ~ ~ ~

Although Lucille's college graduation was only a few months away she was already doing her student teaching. That, combined with a steady social life kept her busy most of the time.

"So, how many boyfriends do you have now?" Millie asked her sister.

Lucille smiled. "Well, let me see. There's Henry and John, and Joe. That's only three for now."

"Unbelievable!" Millie said. "What are you going to do, marry them all?"

"Funny you should ask that," Lucille whispered. "I'm engaged to all three right now."

"What! Are you nuts?"

"No, not really," Lucille laughed. "Think about it. This gives me a chance to really get to know each one of them. Besides they all have jobs elsewhere so they are seldom here at the same time."

Millie snickered, "How do you plan to choose which one to marry?"

"One is rich, one is smart, and one spoils me rotten," she said. "It's hard to choose!"

Millie looked at her sister. "You can't find one with all those qualities?"

"I haven't found him yet," Lucille answered. "A man like that might not exist."

Unfortunately, the families of two of the boys decided, simultaneously to have announcement parties. The telephone rang constantly as both mothers of the intended grooms tried to pin Lucille down to a time and a day when they might announce the engagement.

Anna told Lucille, "You have got to stop this madness, do you understand?" The next time the telephone rang, Anna answered. "I'm so sorry but there won't be any parties, at least not right now. Lucille has decided to wait to set the date until after she graduates and has been teaching for awhile."

The rich one went on a business trip to South America, and the smart one left for Kansas and told Lucille he would continue his studies until she was ready to marry him. That left Joe, who by then owned one of the new automobile convertibles. Everyday at exactly two o'clock in the afternoon, he appeared on the Daigle doorstep, asking Lucille if she wanted to go for a spin around the block.

"Betcha that's the one," Souri told Eliza.

"I think you are right," Eliza said.

Lucille and Joe were married in the house on College Avenue. Eliza was not able to buy material for a wedding dress and Lucille was forced to wear the dress she usually wore for church. When Eliza explained she had no money, her daughter kissed her and said, "It's alright Mama, I'm still married."

~ ~ ~ ~

With Lucille gone, Millie became the oldest of the children still at home and the one to take care of her younger sisters and brother. Lloyd was overjoyed. He had his favorite sister back and

188

gained a second chance to prove to her he could be a good boy. With all his good intentions though, he never quite made it happen. Millie overheard a conversation between Lydia and Rose about a bottle of black cherry wine which Lloyd had made. She knew it was time for Eliza to make her own Cherry Bounce wine which was always opened on Christmas Eve. Determined to get to the bottom of this wine making business, Millie asked Florence about Lloyd's new hobby.

"He showed us how to make cherry wine," Florence said. "It tasted real good."

"I cannot believe this," Eliza said. "He surely has no business making wine for his sisters or for himself! I need every one of those cherries to make my Cherry Bounce. Lord knows that is one of the few things I can make without having to buy anything except sugar!"

Later that same day it became obvious to everyone Eliza had talked to Lloyd because the door to his room was closed, and he did not come downstairs for supper.

That night, Lydia and Rose woke Florence. "Did you tell anyone about the wine?" they asked.

"Yes," Flo answered. "Millie made me tell her and she told Mama."

"Oh, no," Rose gasped, "the Loup Garou. He will probably come tonight and scratch on the window of the person who is a tattletale."

Florence looked at Rose and Lydia with terror in her eyes. The girls huddled beneath the covers. Suddenly, at the window which overlooked College Avenue, there was a soft scrapping noise which grew louder after a few seconds.

"What was that?" Florence whispered.

"I don't know," Rose whispered. "Maybe a branch rubbing the window."

"There aren't any bushes in the front of the house," Lydia gasped.

Oscar and Eliza bolted for the front bedroom as soon as they heard the shrill screams of the girls. Loud sobbing came from underneath the bed, and when Oscar looked, he found his youngest daughters buried in each other's arms.

"What's happening here?" he growled. "You better have a good reason for waking up the entire house!"

"It's Loup Garou, Papa!" Florence cried out. "He's scratching on the window!"

"Come out from under the bed," Oscar said. "There is no such thing as Loup Garou."

Reluctantly, the girls climbed back into bed. The lights were turned off and the house grew quiet once again. The only one still awake was Lloyd. The next day, as Eliza said her morning prayers she added, "Tell me again, Lord. Why did you send me all these children?"

~ ~ ~ ~

By the mid thirties the President's New Deal policy was underway, and many Lafayette men had found work in the WPA, paving the country roads which criss-crossed Lafayette. One of these roads cut right through Oscar's plantation. Almost immediately he received requests from people to buy the land. It intrigued him that he could sell land at a time like this and actually make more money than he could farming, so he decided to divide some of the plantation into small tracts of land.

"I think we have something here, Cher," he told Eliza. "Apparently people really want the land, to farm I suppose, or maybe to raise cattle."

"But Oscar, you can't sell Eagle Crest!" Eliza said.

"I don't intend to sell it all. I'll keep some of it for us and for the workers, but this could bring in enough money to get us through this depression."

"Is that what you want?" Eliza asked him, looking straight into his eyes. "You are taking away our future!"

"We need the money," he answered. "Without money we have no future."

Eliza picked up her rosary, and sitting in her rocker, she began to pray. As her hands slipped along the beads she whispered 'Hail Marys' and 'Our Fathers' in rapid succession and tried to shut her mind to the dangers in Oscar's decision. The ringing telephone caught her by surprise, and her hands shook as she answered it.

Anna's voice bubbled out of the receiver. "Oh, Mama, you were right. I did meet someone yesterday, at a summer party. When he looked at me, and I looked at him, well, it was just wonderful. His name is Edgar. I know now that it was the right thing to do, going to school in Baton Rouge, I mean. It was just the change I needed to meet someone like that."

During the fall of that year Edgar called Anna and within a few months they were engaged. Then it happened again, like it always did. Life came in bunches. George announced he had met his future wife and would be married within a month and Ida gave birth to her first child after fourteen years of marriage. As Souri said, the family really had another layer of kids and people now.

When Eliza's friend Madeline heard that Anna Daigle was to be married to a bank vice-president, she immediately paid a visit to

191

Eliza. Madeline was dressed in a light blue, silk dress and on her head she wore a hat made entirely of brilliant peacock feathers.

"You certainly look nice, Madeline," Eliza said, "and I see you managed to buy not only a new dress, but also a new hat. How many pigs did you give for the new clothes?"

"Oh, my dear," Madeline gushed, "the most wonderful thing has happened. Let's sit in the parlor so we can talk!"

Eliza fingered one of the peacock feathers. "All right," she said, "tell me how you were able to buy these clothes?"

"Well, my dear," she began, "I know you don't have money to buy material for Anna's wedding dress. I think I have the perfect solution to your problem. Do you remember that strange man who opened up the new department store downtown? We called him a French-speaking foreigner? He graciously allowed me to give him a check for all my beautiful clothes and he told me he would hold the check until the bank could make it good. Why, I couldn't believe it, and I asked him outright if this was a joke because no one had ever done that before! He told me he wasn't worried because he knew the bank would cover my check very soon. Before I left the store, he showed me this stunning hat and asked if I might like to buy it also. Of course, you know I did! And he took that check too!"

Eliza had been listening very carefully. "How did you find out about this?" she asked.

"There's a sign in his window right now!" Madeline replied. "Go and see for yourself."

The next morning Eliza went downtown to the department store, and sure enough, there was a sign in the window, "Will Accept Checks Drawn On Any Local Bank." She saw a full bolt of navy blue lace sitting on a table just inside the front door. She did not have any bank checks because Oscar did not believe in using checks to pay for things, but she had written an IOU and was hoping that would be enough.

"May I help you," a small lady asked.

"Yes," Eliza answered, "I would like to buy twelve yards of that navy lace. The only problem is I have no checks, but I do have an IOU. Will you take that?"

The lady took the IOU and disappeared into the back of the store. Eliza fingered the beautiful lace. What a good dress this would make for Anna, she thought. But maybe I should not buy such fine fabric. Madeline is a bad influence on me, just as Oscar said. Still, what harm can there be in just twelve yards? If the owner will accept an IOU then I will pay him as soon as I can. But what would Oscar say if he knew?

"Mr. Rothstein gave me his approval to sell you twelve yards," the lady replied as she began to cut the lace. "He said you must try to pay for the fabric as soon as possible."

Eliza wrapped her arms around the brown package and hurried home, slipping past the front door minutes before Oscar arrived. She quickly opened her armoire and buried the package underneath a blanket.

As her wedding day approached, Anna moved back home. "Just for a few days of course," she said. Edgar often drove in to meet her and Eliza and Oscar liked him right away. Edgar was older than Anna, but he was also vice-president of a prestigious bank in Baton Rouge and this seemed to eliminate most of the objections to the marriage.

After supper, on the night before the wedding, Anna slipped her arms around Oscar's waist and whispered, "Papa! I have a marvelous surprise for you!" She led her father outside, through the front yard to College Avenue where her automobile was parked. As she handed him the keys she said, "This is yours now. I won't be needing it anymore."

Oscar was speechless, and Eliza had a hard time controlling her laughter. "Anna," Eliza said, "do you know the one and only time your father drove a car he yelled "Whoa," instead of pressing on the brake?"

"I know all that, Mama," she replied, "but this will do him good. He can't go on forever riding a horse or driving a wagon behind a horse."

Through sheer determination and under the watchful eye of an overworked guardian angel, Oscar safely drove his family to Anna's wedding. As Eliza stepped out of the shiny black Ford, she whispered to Millie, "miracles do happen."

~ ~ ~ ~

Now that George was married and living away, Millie never received any news about Martin. Every day she thought about the times she sat with him on the front porch and they talked for hours, smiling at one another and holding hands. Millie was still living with Eliza and Oscar although she was now a student at the university. When the annual spring dance came along she accepted the invitation of a friend and decided that Martin had probably forgotten her.

"Wow! You are gorgeous!" Lydia gasped as she saw Millie dressing for the dance. "Who is the new one?"

"I met him in one of my classes," Millie answered. "His name is James."

As soon as Lydia heard the first knock she ran down the hall and, pulling the parlor curtain aside she squealed, "James is here!"

"Good afternoon, sir," James said as Oscar opened the front door. "I am James Lawson. I'm here to take Miss Millie to the university dance."

Oscar eyed him and then said, "Come in. I'll see if Millie is ready."

Oscar and Eliza watched as James held the door of his new Model T for Millie. "He seems like a nice boy," Oscar said. "What about Martin?"

Eliza shook her head. "I haven't heard about Martin in a long time, and that's probably good because I don't think he is the right one for Millie?"

"Why not?" Oscar asked.

"Because he is not like us. He's Spanish and not French! Oh, I don't know how to explain it but I'm glad she is giving someone else a chance."

When Millie got to the dance she saw Martin taking admission tickets. "Do you know that person?" Millie whispered to James.

"Yes," James replied. "Do you know him?"

"No," Millie said. "I was just curious, that's all."

Martin watched Millie the entire night. She was so uncomfortable that she told James she was not feeling well and asked him to take her home.

"I hope it is nothing I have done, Millie?" he asked as he walked her to the front door of her house.

"Oh no, not at all. I had a wonderful time," she answered. "I think I am just tired."

The telephone at the Daigle house rang early the next morning. Rose answered and soon knocked on Millie's door with the message that Martin wanted to speak to her. He told her how glad he was to see her last night. "You look wonderful," he said. He told her about his classes at the university, and that he was studying to be an engineer. Finally he ended by saying he wanted to see her again.

Eliza watched as the relationship between Millie and Martin grew closer. She told her daughter, "He is not like us," and Millie said she was prejudiced against people who were not French. Eliza tried a different argument. "Do you really want to spend the rest of your life with him?" she asked Millie.

"Mama, how is it that you don't object to Anna's choice of a boyfriend?" Millie responded. "He is much older."

"I want you to be happy," Eliza said. "You have so much to offer a man. I wonder if Martin realizes what a treasure he has."

After only a few months, Martin asked Millie to marry him. "He wants to wait until he finishes college and starts a business of his own," she said. "He wants to build a house for me so that we can move into our own home as soon as we marry. Do you remember how you felt when Papa built this house for you?"

"Yes," Eliza answered. "I will never forget how that felt."

Millie took her mother's hand. "Then how can you say he is not the one for me?"

"I don't think I can say that anymore," Eliza answered.

~ ~ ~ ~

Eliza was not surprised when Rose told her she wanted to become a nun. "Do you miss Hilda?" Eliza asked. "Is that the reason you want to be a nun, to be with Hilda?"

196

"That would be nice," Rose answered, "but in the convent I don't get to choose who I will be with."

"Then can you tell me why you want to become a nun?" Eliza continued.

"Because I think that is the only place I will be happy," she answered.

Eliza thought for a moment, and then said, "You have been invited to a party. Are you going?"

"Yes," Rose answered, "I promised Beth I wouldn't miss her birthday. I won't stay that long."

When the day for the party arrived a white limousine pulled up to the house with a driver dressed like a man Eliza once saw in a magazine, all in black with white gloves and a little black hat on the top of his head.

"Hey, Mom!" Lloyd said, holding back the parlor curtain. "I think the President just pulled up to the house. Were you expecting him?"

Eliza laughed. "You know that's for Rose. Stop teasing her!"

Lloyd whistled as he watched Rose climb into the limousine. "All I've got to say is nuns don't drive around in a car like that, and nuns don't look like that either!"

Eliza watched the clock during the time that Rose was at the party. Shortly after the hands of the clock marked the end of the party, Rose burst through the front door, and running down the hall she grabbed her mother and hugged her. "Oh, Mama! I had such a good time! I met someone at the party. He told me he had to be careful because a man could fall in love with a girl like me."

Eliza glanced at Lloyd. "Who is he?" she asked.

"His name is Larry, and he is Beth's cousin. He works at the airport, in the tower, and knows all about airplanes. He's a little

197

older," Rose continued, "but just a little bit, and he has been married before." Rose held her mother's hand. "Oh, Mama, don't judge him without knowing him!"

Eliza realized that Rose suddenly looked different. She was happy. "Does this mean you will postpone entering the convent?" Eliza asked.

"Yes, I think that will be best," Rose answered.

Lloyd started to chuckle. "Postpone? I'd say cancel!"

Eliza took a deep breath. "It will take some time to get used to this new situation. One minute we're contemplating another nun in the family and now we might have another wedding!"

"Mama," Lloyd said, "there is something I have to tell you about Florence."

Eliza looked at him and said, "What now?"

"She met someone at the movie theater today. We see him every time we go there because he takes in the tickets. Well, this afternoon he got someone to take his place so he could sit with her. He bought her some popcorn and a candy bar, and then he asked her for a date. She said no, and then he asked if he could come over here, and she said yes."

Eliza sat back in her porch chair and looked out over the moonlit front yard. The camphor trees threw dancing shadows across the grass. The newly paved street sparkled just enough to mark the way for the handful of automobiles driving along College Avenue.

"What are you thinking about?" Lloyd asked his mother.

Eliza laughed. "I am not thinking. I am praying!"

~ ~ ~ ~

By now the depression had earned the title, "Great." Another world war had begun in Europe and several more banks in Lafayette closed their doors. The money Oscar received from his crops dwindled to almost nothing and it was during this time of great uncertainty and fear that he turned once again to his land.

"It's time for me to sell some more of the plantation," Oscar said. "We are running out of money, and I cannot stand the hardship this will place on you and the children."

Eliza's eyes filled with tears. "This will be very hard for you to do."

Oscar nodded. "I have no other choice. Several people have already offered good money for even a small piece of Eagle Crest."

"How much of the land will you sell this time?" Eliza asked.

Oscar put his arms around Eliza. "I can't sell all of the land along the highway. We will have to keep some of it to allow us access to our first house and the pastures and fields that surround it. I cannot sell the land where the workers live. These parts of Eagle Crest will never be sold, at least not in my lifetime."

Eliza felt a deep sadness settle in her heart and even money from the land could not erase it. Now the memories of Eagle Crest were all she had left.

~ ~ ~ ~

Rose was married in the Daigle house on College Avenue. All the family was there, much to the surprise of Eliza. She decided later that Rose had been the mystery child. No one was sure what would happen to the pretty little girl who always seemed sad. Soon after Rose's wedding Oscar and Eliza learned that Lydia planned to marry the older man who often visited her. This one will not be easy, Eliza thought to herself. All she knew about this man was that he was German, had been married before, and had several children by that marriage.

"Mama, don't worry so much about me," Lydia said. "I know what I am doing, and although I always called him my villain, he is really very sweet."

Eliza knew Oscar didn't like him. "He is too old for her," he told Eliza, "and I don't like the fact that he visits in the dark, in the front yard, and won't even come inside to shake my hand." Eliza also knew there was no way to change Lydia's mind.

After Lydia was married, Eliza couldn't decide if it was her concern for her daughter's happiness which gave her the feeling of having a rock in her stomach, or was it the fact that she didn't know very much about the man Lydia had chosen. "I will just have to place this one in God's hands," she said to Oscar. "They are now husband and wife, and there is nothing we can do about it." Oscar was certain the marriage would not last, or if it did, he said it would most certainly be an unhappy one.

A Most Compromising Situation

The seasons were beginning to change, and there was a hint of winter in the wind now as it moved through the trees. Millie could hear Eliza's rocker creaking against the porch floor. She leaned over and watched her mother's face move in and out of the shadows.

"Mama, have you always trusted Papa?" she asked.

"Yes," Eliza said, "when he was much younger and was seen by a friend in a most compromising situation." Eliza chuckled at the thought of Oscar making a mistake. "You know, of course, your father truly felt he was perfect and could do no wrong."

"Tell me, Mama!" Millie whispered, her eyes sparkling in the darkness.

"Your Papa had gone into town and the horse pulled the surrey over a hole which had a rock in it, and broke one of the wheels. A new school teacher happened to come by in her buggy and she offered Papa a ride to the buggy shop to get the wheel fixed. At first he refused, he said, but she was young and pretty and he finally climbed into her buggy."

"So, what's so bad about that?" Millie asked.

"Nothing's wrong with allowing someone to help," Eliza answered, "but my friend, who just happened to be riding in her own buggy just a few feet away saw Oscar's hand on the woman's knee."

"No! Can't be true!" Millie gasped. "What was his hand doing there?"

"Well, she was driving the buggy so I guess his hand had nothing else to do!"

"Are you sure this is true?" Millie gasped again.

"No, I'm not," Eliza said. "When I asked Oscar about it he looked at me as though I was crazy, and I realized I was making a lot out of nothing. And that was the end of that." Eliza stood up and pushed her rocker against the wall. "Now, I have a question for you," she said. "When are you and Martin getting married?"

Millie sighed. "He has almost finished our house, Mama, and he said as soon as he finishes he will whisk me away to the stars."

"I did not realize you were moving so far away!" Eliza said.

"Oh, Mama, you know our new house is only a few blocks from here!"

By the time the house was finished, Millie had already set the date and Eliza decided to send out invitations well ahead of the wedding day. She said only the closest friends would receive them because they were the only ones who could tolerate so many weddings. As she discussed the invitation with the printer she felt a little catch in her throat, and although she never dreamed Millie would marry the "hummingbird," Eliza was actually happy for the two of them. After the guests had gone, she held her daughter tightly, and with tears in her eyes said, "I know you will be happy because your marriage will be like mine: Made in heaven."

~ ~ ~ ~

The winter of 1940 set a new record with the temperature plunging to fourteen degrees. A soft blanket of snow covered Lafayette and the trees, stripped of their leaves looked like skeletons hanging on the grey sky. Everyone celebrated New Year's Day inside their homes, huddled around fireplaces and stoves. During the fall of each year, Eliza made her famous Cherry Bounce with wild cherries which grew along the side of the house. By New Year's Day, the potent brew was ready, and there was always a ceremony as the first bottle was opened.

"Papa," Regina called out, "Mama says it is time to open the Cherry Bounce!"

As everyone filed into the parlor, Oscar took the first bottle from the tray and opened it with great flourish. He poured a glass, and tasting it he motioned for everyone to gather around with their glasses. Oscar took a deep breath, and surveying his family he said,

"You have all amazed me. My daughters, you are beautiful and talented. My sons, you are strong and handsome. How is it possible that we are still all together in our home in the city, just as we once were in Eagle Crest? It is as though we were meant to be here today, celebrating another new year. With God's continued blessing, may there be more, and may my children and grandchildren come to understand that all these wonderful things are ours because of the love and vigilance of Eliza, your mother and grandmother." Oscar turned to Eliza. "You are the girl I once pledged my life to, and all the vows I made are still true. I will love and cherish you all the days of my life."

That New Year's Day would have been perfect except for the messenger who brought the news that an important sale of land would not go through because the buyer didn't have enough money. Reading the telegram, Oscar stood up from the dinner table and stormed into the parlor. All of the children sat frozen in their chairs as Eliza followed Oscar down the hall. The parlor door slammed, and Eliza's voice rose to meet Oscar's angry words.

"I should not have trusted him!" Oscar screamed. "He was not from here and I knew he was a crook by the way he talked! I passed up two other sales for that piece on his word that he would pay by the first of the year!"

"Calm down," Eliza demanded. "It does you no good to carry on like this. I'm certain you will have another sale tomorrow for that very piece."

The angry words suddenly stopped, and the door to the parlor opened. Eliza stood in the hallway, her face white with fear. "Jules, Armand, George! Come quickly. Something is wrong with Papa!"

~ ~ ~ ~

Doctor Gilbert was a man about Oscar's age, although he looked much older. His hair was almost snow white now and his face crisscrossed with deep lines, the debris from all the trials and mishaps of his years taking care of other people. Although his wife Madeline was one of Eliza's best friends, he and Oscar shared the same thoughts on the friendship of the two women. "I think my wife visits Eliza way too often," he once said and Oscar agreed. As Gilbert emerged from the bedroom he faced the Daigle children.

"Your father had a mild stroke," Gilbert said. "He is hot headed and stubborn, and sometimes the slightest thing can set off people like that. But I understand he also had several glasses of Cherry Bounce, and that, combined with his temper is probably what did him in."

"Do you think he drinks too much?" Eliza asked.

"Well, in this case it was too much," Gilbert replied. "But don't worry, he will have to control his temper and his drinking from here on out. If he doesn't, another stroke will kill him and I've told him so."

In the months which followed, Oscar's stubborn nature gave way to Eliza's careful insistence that he eat the right foods and stay away from alcohol all together. Oscar began to mellow and despite a strict diet which completely eliminated his favorite dinner of round steak and rice and gravy, he remained cheerful, and sometimes downright pathetic.

"Cher, please get me a little tobacco for my pipe," he said, "to help me in my misery."

Eliza took his pipe and disappeared down the hall, into the place where she hid his tobacco. When she returned with the filled pipe, Oscar looked up at her and asked, "What am I having for supper, Cher?"

"The usual," she replied, "spinach and chicken breast, with a big glass of sauerkraut juice."

Oscar's illness brought the family closer together and as his strength slowly returned Oscar was faced with giving away his last daughter. Florence and the boy she met at the movie theater were married.

Regina spent long hours with her father, perhaps to reconnect with her childhood and to confirm that he alone was her only way to explain why she existed. During those visits they talked often about Regina's birth, and the two of them decided it was time to choose one of the children to share the secret. When Regina discussed this with Eliza, she learned her mother had already made a choice.

"What made you decide that Jules was the one?" Regina asked.

"He is the one who will understand the situation," Eliza replied. "I will tell Jules when he and Papa come back from the visit to Doctor Gilbert and I'll make sure he knows this is our secret, his, mine and Papa's. After we die, he can tell another one of the children or he can tell all of them at once."

Eliza led Jules into the kitchen and sat him down at the kitchen table, just as she had done when he was a little boy. "Mama, are you going to make a cup of coffee for me out of milk and sugar, like you used to do?" Jules asked.

Eliza laughed. "No, this will be a real cup of coffee." She looked at his face. In many ways he looked like Oscar, with his light eyes and dark hair, but she always thought he was more handsome than his father.

Eliza took a sip of her coffee. "Jules, there is something I have to tell you. But before I tell you I want you to understand that this has been a secret between Regina, Papa, and me for many years." Jules sat back in his chair and frowned. Eliza continued. "Before Papa met me he was married to Regina's mother. She died giving birth to Regina, and Papa asked his own mother, Grandma Daigle to help him take care of his baby."

Jules stirred his coffee and then looked up at his mother. "I always wondered why Regina looked so much like Papa. I guess this explains it."

"Regina herself did not know for quite a while," Eliza said. "She discovered who her real mother was during the time she attended school as a boarder. Regina's mother was a Boudreau, and one of her nieces went to school with Regina. This girl knew the story and told Regina."

"How did she take this?" Jules asked.

"At first she was very angry with your father and me, but Papa told her it was his decision to wait until she was older. He admitted he waited too long."

"What do you want me to do with this?" Jules asked.

Eliza reached out and touched his hand. "Regina wants you to wait to tell anyone else, and Papa and I agree with her. There is nothing to be gained by telling the others now. I trust you. You will know when the time is right."

"Well, Mama," Jules said, "you have given me much to think about."

"Thank you son," Eliza said with tears in her eyes. "You have lifted a burden from my shoulders."

As Jules stood up to leave, he reached into his coat pocket and pulled out an envelope. "Here Mama, this is to help with the medical expenses for Papa. I don't want you to worry about that, at least!"

Oscar continued to improve and the real test came when he was able to turn down a sale for the rest of the land along the highway. "This is where my life started," he said, "and where all my children were born. Eagle Crest will belong to them one day."

~ ~ ~ ~

There was no doubt in Oscar's mind that Lloyd would be the one to make the plantation successful once again. After his high school graduation Lloyd moved to Baton Rouge to study horticulture. Before long he fell in love with a girl on campus and brought his future bride to Eliza's annual birthday celebration. The talk around the table that evening was about the entry of the United States into World War II. When it became obvious that Lloyd had decided to enter the military, Eliza's heart sank. She knew all the reasons for the war but none justified the possible loss of one of her children to a cause she did not fully understand. It was Eliza's firm belief if everyone did what God wanted, there would be no wars. Oscar went to bed early that evening and when Eliza came into the bedroom, he saw tears in her eyes.

"How was your birthday, Cher?" he asked.

"It was a beautiful day," Eliza answered, "except for Lloyd's discussion about the war. When he said he may be stationed in Europe, I felt my heart break."

Oscar gently kissed her hand. "Don't worry. He is only doing what he thinks is right. After all, this is not necessarily a death sentence. The army told him he will probably be assigned as an interpreter and possibly an aid to General Eisenhower. I am certain

Lloyd will be well taken care of. Besides, since he is the baby of this family he is probably looking forward to seeing the world from a different perspective."

CHAPTER NINETEEN

THE GREAT DEPRESSION was over and the economy grew strong gradually. New banks opened and the farmers and city workers, teachers and doctors had money once again. Oscar saw the plantation awaken from its long sleep and he was glad he had kept the rest of the land. All the workers returned except one. His friend Joseph had passed away, and even though Joseph's son, Jefferson was there to carry on the work of his father, the connection between the past and the present for Oscar was lost forever.

"He and I were almost the same age," Oscar told Eliza. "At times he was my brother, at other times my friend, but never was he my slave. Because of Joseph, I will always have the highest respect for the men and women who work for Eagle Crest. They take care of the land and it takes care of them. The simplicity in that should be a lesson for all of us."

"I will miss Pappy," Souri said as she and Oscar placed Joseph's headstone next to Isabel's. "But I know he is with Momma and my brother and William now. That's all that counts."

"Will you go back to the plantation?" Eliza asked her.

"No, not now, Miss Eliza," Souri replied. "I still got you and Mr. Oscar to care for. Maybe someday, though, when no one needs me anymore."

Two Fish

Perhaps it was the fact that Lloyd was far away now, or maybe it was the rain that late summer morning that caused a feeling of uneasiness in Eliza's heart. When the phone rang she jumped.

"Mama!" George's voice filled Eliza's ear. "How is Papa feeling?"

"Much better," Eliza answered. "How's your family?" George and his wife never visited much, and Eliza tried to remember how old George's two children would be now.

"Today, I'm going fishing with my two buddies at White Lake," George said. "I'll bring you some fresh fish for supper tonight."

"Papa will like that," Eliza laughed. "He would choose fresh fish over chicken any time!"

She hung up, and glanced out the window again. The horizon seemed to be lined with black cotton and she could see lightning dancing across the sky. "How can he fish in this weather?" she wondered. Bad weather always bothered her, and as the day wore on the storm clouds increased her uneasiness. George had promised he would bring the fish in time for supper, but he never came. "Probably got caught in the rain," Eliza whispered, but somehow she knew that was not the reason. The knock on the door brought her the answer.

"Mrs. Daigle?" The sheriff's deputy was a big man with a round belly that hung over his belt like a shelf.

"Yes?"

"Is Mr. Daigle here also?"

"I'm sorry; he has already gone to bed. Is something wrong?"

"Mrs. Daigle, we found a capsized boat belonging to your son George. He was apparently fishing at White Lake and was possibly caught in a tornado. We have not yet found a body and we are hoping he made it to the shore somewhere."

Eliza walked into the parlor and sat down in her rocker in the bay window. The room seemed so close, airless and dark. She leaned back and began to rock, her rosary slipping between her fingers.

"Do you have someone we can call for you?" the deputy asked.

"No," she said, "I will call the children."

The vigil began early the next morning with the arrival of Edward and Jules. All through the day the rest of the children appeared. Finally George's wife arrived, looking frail and tired. The first day disappeared into the next and still no word on survivors. Hope began to diminish and Eliza spent more and more of her time with Oscar, both of them crying softly through the night. On the fourth day two of the bodies were found, and finally on the fifth day, George's body washed ashore. Eliza and Oscar identified their son and took him home.

During the months that followed Eliza understood that time can be an enemy as well as a friend, and although there are many problems solved by its passage, it is a blessing when a death is quick and final. "Do you believe in signs?" she asked Oscar. When he replied he did not think the dead could contact the living, Eliza smiled because she knew differently. After all, she surmised, what is more natural than a child wanting to tell his mother something? When a tiny boy knocked on the door and asked if she would like to buy some fresh fish, Eliza asked, "Where did you catch these?"

"My Papa caught them at White Lake, Ma'am," the child replied.

Waiting on the street was an old man in a wagon. When Eliza looked his way he smiled and waved. "I'll buy two of them from you," she told the child. That night she cooked the fish for Oscar's supper. They were fresh and sweet just as she thought they would be.

"Where did you get these, Cher?" Oscar asked.

"From a child who came to the door," she replied. "His father was waiting in a wagon and I didn't recognize him, but I know who the little boy was."

Farewell to Eagle Crest

During the spring of 1943 Lloyd sent a letter to Eliza and told a story about his adventures in England. She often talked about that letter and kept it on the table next to her rocker in the parlor. She said it was an example of the kind of son Lloyd was.

> Dear Mom and Pop:
>
> I decided to type this one out to you, not that I have that much to tell you, but because I think it is much plainer than my handwriting. I received your letter of April 26th. I am glad you received the flowers for Easter. When you are so far apart you can never be certain that the things you send will reach their destination. I think that was mighty nice of you to give everyone my address. I hope they write. Mail is the only thing that keeps a guy going around here. You asked about Easter over here … well it wasn't so bad. We stayed with a British family. The first night the lady asked me if I wanted a bed partner. I was embarrassed and said no, thank you. The next night the lady brought me a hot water bottle and said, "I thought you might

212

need a bed partner tonight." All joking aside, that really happened. Flo, I wish you would take a few snap shots for me. I want one of Mom and Pop in their victory garden and one of Mom and Pop in front of the house. Take the latter so that it shows a lot of the house. I know what you are saying. "Who the hell does he think he is?" This is it, Flo. A guy gets awful lonesome for his home when he is so far away from it. Mom, you'd better pray for me. I am getting to be a renegade in my spare time. I spend all of it playing cards. It's really not that bad, but I am lonesome for you and Pop.

Love,

Lloyd

When the war ended, Lloyd was asked to stay one more year as Eisenhower's aide, but he turned the offer down and came home. Oscar could see that Lloyd left as a child and returned a man, and he was amazed at his son's transformation. He was eager now to work on the plantation and even talked about living there.

During the winter of that year, a flu epidemic raged in Lafayette. People said it was caused by a winter not cold enough to kill the germs. The hospitals were full and doctors warned the sick to stay home or risk being sent to one of the pest houses to die.

"Eliza, you must keep Oscar home," Gilbert said as he gently shut the bedroom door. "He has the flu, and may be starting with pneumonia. He is still weak from that stroke."

After Eliza heard Oscar's breathing, she called Gilbert, and now he was confirming her worst fear. "But I am afraid," she said. "He seems very sick. How do I take care of him?"

"You must have help," Gilbert replied. "Do you still have Souri?"

"Yes," Eliza said. "Let me get her now and you can tell both of us what to do."

As Eliza walked to the kitchen she remembered those nights with her mother and the way it felt to watch someone die. How could this happen to Oscar? "No!" she whispered. She shook her head. "No! He can't leave me alone now!"

After Gilbert gave the two women their instructions, Eliza brought Souri a washcloth and a basin of cold water. "Sponge him off, please," she said to Souri. "I want to pray. I'll be in the parlor if you need me."

Eliza sat in her rocker. She began to cry and quickly wiped the tears away. She knew she must not give up. She also knew God's will would be done no matter what she wanted, but the frustration of the moment became too much, and sobbing, she buried her head in her hands. "Please keep him safe, dear God. He has my heart, and if his stops beating, then what will I do? Give us a little more time together, please."

"Miss Eliza," Souri called from the hall, "Mr. Oscar is awake and wants to see you."

Eliza walked into the dark bedroom. She could see Oscar in bed. He looked thin and tired. "How are you feeling?" she whispered.

"Very tired," he said, "but I am hungry, Cher. Could I have something to eat?"

Eliza had not heard those words in several days. "Of course," she replied. "What do you want?"

"I would like a little rice and gravy," he answered. "But I guess my diet won't allow that."

Eliza smiled at him. "We'll forget about the diet. Souri, take the surrey and go to the butcher shop. Buy a round steak."

"Yes, Miss Eliza!" Souri said with a smile that stretched all across her face.

Oscar seemed to get better from that night on, although Doctor Gilbert cautioned Eliza not to let him outside. "Pneumonia is a strange thing," he told her. "It sometimes hides."

The weather improved by turning cold in time for Christmas. Lloyd was home from the war and once again the Daigle family gathered around the dining room table. After dinner Oscar was visibly weaker and he told Eliza he wanted to go to bed. "Good night, everyone," he said, "I will see all of you in the morning."

"Papa," Millie said, "let us all give you a kiss, like the old days."

Oscar laughed and sat down again in his chair. "All right then, line up, oldest to youngest."

First in line was Regina, then Edward and Cady, Gabriel, Ida, and Jules. Next was Anna, then Lucille and Armand and Hilda. After Hilda would have been George. Theresa came next, then Mildred, Lydia, and Rose. Florence and Lloyd were the last two children to give their father a kiss good night.

While the women stayed in the dining room, the men took their discussion of the war out to the front porch. "It's not a question of whether the President did the right thing," Jules said. "The question is could we have ended the war with Japan another way?"

Edward leaned up against the porch railing. "I have a question for you, Jules. How should we feel about the Japanese after they forced us into war by attacking Pearl Harbor?"

215

"I don't have an answer to that," Jules replied. "I know what the church teaches, but in reality do most people think we should love our enemies, even if they kill our families and children?"

Lloyd shook his head. "You should have heard what I heard from the Europeans, about the bombing of Nagasaki and Hiroshima. The majority of people were horrified at this terrible force which we used to kill so many innocent people. How should we feel about the Germans?" he asked Jules. "They killed thousands of Jews. How can we pretend they are not murderers? And if we do condemn the Germans, are we condemning our own sister for marrying one?"

~ ~ ~ ~

The cold which enveloped Christmas was still there in January. Long icicles laced the tree branches and the wind, damp and piercing, whistled at the doors and windows like a banshee. Eliza had firewood brought in from the plantation because Oscar's cough seemed to get worse each night as the cold crept through the floors and walls. Soon, she called Dr. Gilbert and asked that he hurry. Oscar was having trouble breathing again.

Eliza propped him up on more pillows, and felt his face. "You have fever," she said. "Here, drink a little water, if you can."

Oscar took a sip then pushed it away and began to cough. He turned and looked at his wife. The light from the setting sun sent a hundred rainbows from the icicles dancing across the room. He reached for her hand and held it to his lips.

"I remember the day I first saw you," he whispered. "You were teaching catechism under the oak. So beautiful. Cher, you will be in charge of the plantation now. Take Lloyd with you each time you go. And when you are ready to come to meet me, give each of the children a piece of Eagle Crest." He coughed again.

"Lie still," Eliza said, "you don't have to talk."

"I have to tell you now," he answered, "because I am dying. Don't cry, Cher. I have had such a good life with you. I loved you instantly when I first saw you and I knew then I would marry you. "

Eliza held his hand to her heart. "It was God's will that we marry," she said. "I'm sure of that because He has guided my every step, and yours too. No matter where you are, I will always love you."

Dr. Gilbert told Eliza to call the children. As she walked to the phone she thought her heart would break in two. "I suppose God needs him now," she whispered. Each time she dialed a number it was with great determination. She made certain it was the right number, and when the voice answered she said what she had to say and hung up. Souri had a cup of coffee waiting for Eliza in the kitchen. She drank the hot coffee slowly, looking out the window at the white trees and lawns.

"Everything will die this winter," Eliza said. "Nothing that is alive can stand this cold."

Souri wiped her eyes. "Can I do something for Mr. Oscar?" she asked.

"No, Souri," Eliza answered, "I need your help."

The children sat around Oscar's bed and listened to his breathing, each one taking a breath for him. It was dark now, and the shadows in the house seemed to be deeper than ever. Eliza took the washcloth which Regina had dipped in cold water and gently wiped her husband's forehead. He appeared to be asleep.

"Why does he sound like that, Mama?" Rose asked.

"That is the death rattle," Eliza answered. "I heard your grandmother breathe just like that."

217

Oscar opened his eyes and looked at each of the children. He began to draw very deep breaths of air. His throat made a hoarse sound and as the children gathered close, he took his last breath with his eyes resting upon Eliza.

Regina walked to the clock which sat on the mantel above the fireplace, and opening the glass door, she stopped the pendulum. The time was ten o'clock. Eliza remembered waking up in her mother's parlor the night Emelie died. Someone had stopped that clock too, and Eliza couldn't understand why. Now she knew the answer. When someone dies time has to stop, for a little while at least, because time is made by people to measure the distance from birth to death.

Eliza held Regina tightly. "Mama," she whispered "I am an orphan now."

~ ~ ~ ~

The chapel of Saint John was now a cathedral and Eliza could see the massive steeple from her front porch. She always made the sign of the cross when she heard the bells ring for a funeral, but today was Oscar's funeral and her heart was full of sadness. It was impossible to pray. She dressed quickly. Maybe the children would need something and she didn't want to be fussing with her hair or her hat. She looked at the bed she shared with Oscar for fifty-three years. The men came too soon to carry him away. She needed more time to wash his face and hands and feet. Instead, she spent those minutes after he died consoling the children. Now she wished she could touch him one more time. Jules was calling her now. He wanted to take her early to the church so she could be with Oscar before the service started.

Eliza walked up to the casket which was placed in front of the altar at the end of the center aisle. She touched Oscar's hands, and then his cheeks. His tie was crooked and she straightened it. Glancing around the Cathedral she saw Madeline and her husband, and sitting behind them was the Smith family. Souri and Jefferson sat in the middle of the church with their sisters and Lucius, and the workers from the plantation. In the front pews, on both sides, were the Daigle children with their wives and husbands and their children. She touched Oscar one more time and then sat down with her family.

The bishop led the procession from the back of the Cathedral. Standing in front of the communion rail he recited the prayers for the dead as he blessed Oscar's body with holy water. The pall bearers shut the casket and the Requiem Mass began. Latin words drifted in and out of Eliza's mind. It was May in Côte Gelée and she and Oscar were dancing. Her parents were there, and Charles was twirling Idea around the dance floor. Eliza had never seen him dance before. Leocade was watching from the hallway, tapping her feet to the music. In her arms she held baby Regina.

"Here is a man whose name may not be scrawled on the front pages of every newspaper in the nation." Eliza looked up. Oscar's brother Francois was at the podium. "But here is a man who lived a truly Christian life. He had many good qualities, and I will mention a few here. This noble man raised seventeen children – sixteen of whom are living – strong men and women whom he has given to the church and to the nation. Five whose lives are consecrated to God, two sons, one a priest and the other a Christian Brother and three daughters, all sisters of a teaching order. And he also gave two sons in the service of their country. The others are all themselves raising families of their own.

219

"This man was not a millionaire and yet he raised seventeen children. We don't know what sacrifices he made. You who find it hard to raise one or two children, can you imagine the sacrifices he and his wife made day after day for so many years? Those countless sacrifices must surely have atoned for his sins and merited for him a place in heaven. What a comfort it must have been to him to spend his last hours surrounded by these loving ones and his faithful wife. How great must be his joy now as he looks down upon them knowing that many, many prayers are being offered for his soul today and that countless more will be offered daily in the time to come."

Eliza and the children, with their families followed the casket out of church and through the St. John cemetery to a spot where she and Oscar had long ago decided they themselves would be buried. Glancing up, Eliza saw the grave diggers sitting on top of a tractor.

She leaned over to Jules. "You must stay behind and make certain everything is done properly. Those men don't look too smart to me."

Jules smiled. "Yes, Mama, I will. Don't worry."

After the burial everyone went to the house on College Avenue, and for the first time in their lives, the children sat around the dining room table without Oscar.

~ ~ ~ ~

After Joseph died, Eliza was certain it was just a matter of time before Souri moved back to the plantation to live in her parents' house. Souri was adamant, however, that she would not leave Eliza until there was absolutely no need for her to stay. "Why, Miss

Eliza, you will just have to up and die before I leave you," Souri often said. "That's the way it's gonna be."

"You are not young anymore," Eliza told her, "and you have your own health to worry about."

"I know that," Souri snapped back. "But that's the way it's gonna be."

Eliza remembered these conversations after she found Souri dead in the kitchen one cold Monday morning. Dr. Gilbert said it was her heart that gave out, just like her father's heart had done. Eliza and Jefferson held the wake for Souri in the front room of Joseph and Isabel's old house, and all the workers and their children came to mourn the little black woman who would always be a part of Eagle Crest. Eliza and Jefferson wanted to bury her next to her parents, but a big root from the old oak was in the way, so they put her off to the right, with her grave facing the east.

"That's good," Jefferson said. "She can watch the sun come up in the morning. That was always her favorite time of the day."

Lloyd and Millie decided to take turns helping Eliza now that Souri was gone. Lloyd went to visit his mother every morning and sat with her in the kitchen for a cup of coffee. Millie went every afternoon to take Eliza shopping or help her around the house. It was Lloyd who first suspected that Eliza was not feeling well, and he called Millie. Together they decided to call Doctor Gilbert. "Don't you know when someone breathes like that, they have pneumonia?" Gilbert told them. "Your father sounded just like that."

"But Papa was very sick," Millie replied. "Mama does not seem sick at all. She has not said a word about feeling bad."

"I realize that," Gilbert said, shaking his head, "but she does have fever and she told me her chest hurts. I suppose she didn't want to worry you. However, we have seen a lot of pneumonia this winter, especially in the older ones," he continued. "For that reason, I have the new penicillin drug with me. Oscar was not so lucky. He died before this was discovered."

Gilbert walked back into Eliza's bedroom. "You have a touch of pneumonia, I'm afraid," he told her. "I'm going to give you a shot of penicillin today, and probably another one tomorrow. We will see how that works."

"I've heard about that," Eliza said. "What is it?"

Gilbert smiled at her question. "It is a medicine made from a particular kind of mold," he answered. "It is considered the miracle drug of the century, and its power was discovered just in time to help you."

Eliza eyed the doctor as he rolled up the sleeve of her dress. "You know very well how I feel about this sort of thing, don't you?"

"Yes, yes," he answered, "I do, but you are sick and you must get well."

"I believe the human body has all it needs to cure itself. Medicine is just a poison."

"Remember, my dear, you are seventy-two years old, by my calculations at least, and this illness could be very hard on you. Don't worry your children and me by starting a fuss over taking medicine."

Eliza turned her head as Gilbert injected the penicillin into her arm. She did not see Millie and Lloyd smile as they watched the doctor tape a gauze pad over the tiny red prick in her skin. Gilbert told her to try to sleep, and to stay inside out of the wind and cold for at least seven days.

After the penicillin injections, Eliza's health improved rapidly and when the letter from the bishop arrived, she announced the message it contained with a great deal of excitement. The letter began with congratulations and then the bishop informed her that she would receive the Papal Medal from Rome. "That is the highest medal the Pope can give anyone," she said.

The news of Eliza's honor spread quickly and the local radio station asked Eliza for an interview. She was astounded at the request because she believed that the invention of the radio was a miracle. When Oscar brought home the first one she sat for hours listening to everything from the news about the war, to stories told by people she could not even see. "This is incredible!" she whispered over and over, adding, "Someday I want someone to explain to me how this works."

During the drive to the radio station Lloyd told his mother how radio was discovered. After listening carefully, she seemed satisfied and her only comment was, "It is truly a miracle because a man could not make this without God's help."

Lloyd smiled at the predictability of that observation. "Are you nervous?" he asked.

"No," she replied. "Should I be?"

As he stopped the car in the station parking lot, he looked at her. "Remember everyone is going to be listening to you. Have you practiced what you will say?"

"No," Eliza sighed. "I will rely on the Holy Ghost to give me the right words."

The studio was cold and quiet, not at all like she imagined, and when the producer motioned for her to take a seat in front of the microphone, she looked around for whatever that would be.

"Here we are Mrs. Daigle," he said, pulling a chair out from under the table which held the microphone.

"Is that it?" she asked as she sat down.

"Yes, Mama, that's it," Lloyd said, trying not to smile.

The producer turned his own chair towards Eliza. "Now Mrs. Daigle, I want you to relax and just answer my questions in your regular voice. You do not have to talk loudly. The microphone is very sensitive."

Eliza folded her hands and sat back in the chair. She was not even aware of the red light above the door which read, "On the Air." She smiled slightly as the interview began.

"Good evening. You are listening to KVOL Radio, Lafayette. We have with us in the studio a wonderful mother and useful citizen of our community, Mrs. Oscar Landry Daigle of 705 West College Avenue. She was born seventy-two years ago in Côte Gelée, which is now Broussard. In 1893, she married Oscar G. Daigle, who took her to begin their new life together in Lafayette. Now, 55 years later, she has memories to look back upon such as few women will ever obtain. It is with pride now that she can say that every one of her seventeen children was reared in the Catholic faith in Catholic schools. Every one of them received a college education, and five of them have been given to the service of God. Tell us, Mrs. Daigle, about your remarkable family."

Eliza sat up, and looked steadily at Lloyd. "People are surprised when they hear about my seventeen children. They don't understand how I could have borne the hardships and trouble that it took. Well, I guess in my day we just prayed differently. We used to pray to God to give us the strength to bear our troubles and burdens. Today the mothers just pray not to have any troubles. They throw away their crosses and so they throw away the greatest happiness a woman can know. If mothers of today would only realize the joy it brings to have the love of children. It is heaven on earth to grow old knowing that you have so many young people to love and to have so much to be interested in. I don't know what I would live for now if it were not for my children. I thank God for every one of them."

CHAPTER TWENTY

THE YEARS HAVE a way of redefining the things which are important in the lives of people. When the Chapel of St. John became a cathedral, everyone said how glorious the huge bell sounded as it echoed across the city. Many years before, when the little bell of the chapel rang it filled the air with a soft melody and people stopped what they were doing to listen. Now, time itself was governed by noise. Each day at noon, a shrill whistle blew from the rooftop of City Hall, and bank presidents and managers closed their office doors, workers put their hammers and shovels to rest, and everyone sat down to eat lunch. For one hour the city was quiet, then the busses and cabs resumed their rounds and each minute was filled with noise once again.

When Eliza and Oscar first sat on the porch of their new house on College Avenue, they could see for miles in every direction, and at night they could hear the hushed conversations of the neighbors across the street. Now, when the wind blew from the north, Eliza could hear the wheels of the trains clicking along the new railroad tracks. Oscar was so excited when the railroad was built, but to Eliza the noise of the railroad cars meant winter was on the way. Eliza spent less and less time on the front porch. Her days began and ended with walks to the Cathedral for Mass and visits to the Blessed Sacrament. With all the traffic she found it difficult to cross College Avenue, but she was determined to continue these daily trips until, she said, God showed her another way to visit Him.

Eliza stopped waiting for Oscar to return. She no longer listened for his footsteps down the hall. She no longer thought she heard someone call her name. By now, Eliza knew that some things did not happen by accident and that a strange occurrence was not necessarily just a coincidence. She felt all of these things were messages from God.

She talked to Oscar a lot about the grandchildren and the funny things they did and said. She was certain he heard her stories because those grandchildren were the next generation from Eagle Crest. Holidays without Oscar became a bittersweet reminder that Eliza's life had changed. As the years slipped by, the house on College Avenue always seemed full of children and grandchildren. This was especially true for Christmas Day. "Hey y'all," they called out to one another. "*Comment ça va?*" Someone always answered, "*Ça va bien!* We're doing great! *Et vous?*" Soon the parlor floor around the Christmas tree was piled high with presents. When the grandchildren saw Eliza leave the kitchen and walk down the hall toward the parlor they all ran to her, pulling on her dress and begging to open their presents.

After dinner and all the presents were opened, Eliza served coffee in tiny demi tasse cups, each one different with matching saucers edged in gold. As Eliza walked with the coffee tray she waded through a sea of coloring books and paper dolls, model airplanes, jacks, books and toy guns.

Jules handed each niece and nephew a silver dollar, telling them, "If you continue to be good, I will increase it every year. Then you will be rich!"

Once, when it was almost time to go home, the grandchildren decided someone should climb the wall which separated Eliza's yard from the monastery next door. It was not an easy decision to

227

make because Eliza told each one of them that the good Sisters who lived on the other side of the wall wished to be left alone. "That is the purpose of the wall," she said. But the question that particular day was: "Why would anyone want to live behind a wall when there was so much to see and do on the outside?"

"Who wants to climb the wall?" Lloyd's daughter Lois Gail asked.

"Florence's son Ronnie decided to warn his cousins. "Of course you all know what will happen as soon as someone looks at the Sisters."

"What?" everyone gasped.

"We will all go to hell," he answered.

Lois Gail shook her head. "That's not true! Who told you that?"

"Grandma," Ronnie said solemnly, "and you know she's always right!"

Lois Gail fingered the purple wisteria vine which grew up against the concrete wall. "I can climb this – watch." She put her foot into the first fork in the heavy trunk, and holding onto the vine she climbed halfway up before looking down to find Ronnie, and Millie's daughter, Connie, on their way up also. The vine branched out at that point and Lois Gail was able to climb side-ways now, making room for her cousins on the other branches. In just a few minutes all three children were peering over the wall. In the monastery courtyard three nuns were on their knees in the dirt, their habits flattened out around them in great pools of white.

"What are they doing?" Lois Gail whispered.

"I don't know," Ronnie answered. "Maybe they lost some-thing."

Standing on the topmost branch of the vine, Connie listened intently. The only sounds from the courtyard were a series of soft clicking noises followed by the muffled conversation of the nuns. Because of the time of the day there was little traffic on College Avenue.

"I think they are playing marbles," Connie whispered.

Lois Gail looked at Ronnie and laughed. "She's right! Look at them!"

Climbing down quickly the threesome had barely set foot on Eliza's grass when she appeared.

"What are you all doing out here?" Eliza asked, her voice dripping with suspicion. When she received no answer she told them they must now pray very hard for forgiveness.

~ ~ ~ ~

Eliza's daily walk to church became more difficult. She told Millie that the automobiles had to stop to let her cross, and she could feel her heart pounding away in her chest as she tried to walk faster. Millie suggested the house should be sold. "We'll buy another one for you, right next to the church," she said. Eliza wondered if she could give up the house Oscar had built for her. Before long the answer to her question came in the form of a business card stuck in the crack of her front door. "Can't hurt to call this person," she whispered as she dialed the number on the card.

After a few moments, a voice said, "Daniel Pierce, may I help you?"

"Yes," Eliza answered, "my name is Eliza Daigle, and I own the house at 705 College Avenue. You left a card in my door."

229

"Yes, Mrs. Daigle," Pierce replied. "I am certainly glad to hear from you. I would like to visit with you, perhaps tomorrow? There is a large company called Sears and Roebuck which would like to locate here. The company is interested in your property."

After hanging up Eliza immediately called Millie and Lloyd and asked them both to join her for the meeting. Millie said she would bring Martin, and Lloyd said he thought Jules should be present also. When Eliza told Jules about possibly selling the house there was a long silence.

"Mama, are you sure about this?" he asked. "Wouldn't you like to stay there and have one of us come to pick you up for church?"

"That would be wonderful," she replied, "but that is a lot to ask."

"I know, I know," Jules answered. "You want to be next to the church, but I think you will miss your house."

Eliza didn't sleep well that night. There were so many memories. Like a tapestry they hung in the rooms and hallways of her mind – Oscar and his Eagle Crest, rainbows over the pastures, moonlight in the cotton fields, rockers on the front porch in the city, Souri and babies, laughter and tears, and promises. In the darkness Eliza realized this was the fabric of her life.

The group listened intently as Daniel Pierce explained that Sears and Roebuck was expanding their department stores into Louisiana. Eliza's property together with the adjacent land of the monastery was perfect for the new store, and Pierce asked if Eliza would be willing to sell.

"I want to make myself clear, Mr. Pierce," Eliza answered. "I do think the time will come very soon when I am unable to cross College Avenue safely in order to get to church. The money would be nice also. I don't need it, but I think it would make a nice gift to my children. However, I do not want to give up the house because my husband built it for me, and it has become a part of my life."

"Have you ever thought of having this house moved, Mrs. Daigle?" Pierce asked.

"Is that possible?" she replied.

Pierce smiled and said, "I think so."

After Pierce left, Jules motioned for Lloyd and Martin to walk outside. It was five o'clock and the number of automobiles on College Avenue amazed the three men. Jules gestured toward the street. "If Mama continues to live here she will need our help everyday to cross the street. Moving the house is the only answer. It will have to be somewhere close to church," Jules continued, "on the same side of St. John Street as the church, and we will need a lot big enough to hold the whole house. Mama would never leave any piece of it behind."

Millie pushed aside the curtains of the bay windows and watched the three men in the front yard. "Mama, are you sure you want to do this?"

"What choice do I have?" Eliza replied. "I am an old woman and I do not want to put myself in danger. I suppose I could sell the house with the property, but I don't think I will be happy with that."

~ ~ ~ ~

A large lot with an old house came up for sale near the Cathedral. Within two weeks the old house was moved away and Eliza's house was moved in its place. Now, when she looked out of her kitchen window Eliza could see the back of the church and a corner of the old graveyard. She lost no time in putting on her

231

new hat and white gloves and walking all the way to the church without having to cross a single street. She sat in her pew and made the sign of the cross. "Thank you God," she whispered, "for helping me to find my way once again."

There were many times Eliza wondered if all the memories would follow the house to the new address, or would some be swallowed up like the camphor trees, the rose bushes, the old potato shed and the wine cellar. Not long after Eliza was settled at the new address, the children decided their mother should have a television set. "We'll buy it from Sears and Roebuck," Lloyd said. "You are going to love this, Mama!"

"But how does it work?" Eliza asked.

"Remember how amazed you were at radio?" he asked. "Television works like that; only a television set receives pictures from the air as well as sounds."

"That's incredible!" she answered. "Is it dangerous?"

Lloyd laughed. "No, Mama! Is radio dangerous?"

"I'm not sure," Eliza replied. "It doesn't seem too good when all these things are flying through the air."

Eliza ran her hand across the strange looking box which now sat in the parlor. "Well, turn it on," she told Lloyd. As the picture appeared, she pulled her rocker up close to it and folded her hands in her lap. "It's not very clear," she said, "and please turn up the sound. You know I can't hear well."

"Mama, you are sitting too close!" Lloyd said.

Eliza sighed as she repositioned herself and then gazed in amazement at the screen, glancing at Lloyd and then looking back at the strangers talking to her. "Incredible," she whispered over and over again.

A Time to Rest

Millie watched the reflection of the overhead lights form stepping stones along the hospital corridor which led to Eliza's room. "Twenty, twenty-one, twenty-two, twenty-three," she whispered. There were twenty-three lights between the entrance to the hospital and room 115. "Mama," she said, knocking softly, "it's me."

Millie pushed open the door. The room was in darkness except for a small light over the head of the bed. Eliza was asleep, her hands folded across her chest. The monitor showed a steady heart beat. "Mama, how do you feel?" Millie whispered.

Eliza turned her head. Her eyes rested on Millie's face and she smiled. "Such a shame to give you so much trouble," she answered.

Millie stroked her mother's cold face. Not more than a few seconds ago, it seemed, Millie had gone shopping for her mother. "Buy some good peaches," Eliza said, "and I'll make peach preserves." Millie left her working in the front yard, cleaning out the flowers which had been scorched by the August heat. When Millie returned Eliza was in bed. "I am just tired," she said. "I am an old lady, you know."

"Does anything hurt?" Millie asked.

Eliza rubbed her arms. "My arms ache. I think I pulled a muscle somewhere."

Millie looked at her mother carefully. "I think we should go to the hospital and have someone look at you. Can you sit up?"

Eliza tried to move but each time she became short of breath and fell back into the bed. By the time she was admitted to the hospital Eliza knew she was gravely ill but she never suspected a heart attack. She listened as Dr. Gilbert whispered instructions to the nurses and must have slept a little because she awoke to the sound of voices. Why, that's Edward, she thought, and Lloyd, and Anna. She opened her eyes. The lights were very dim.

"What time is it?" Eliza whispered.

"My dear, dear lady," Dr. Gilbert answered, "it is time for you to rest."

"What is wrong with me?" Eliza asked.

Gilbert cradled her hands in his. "You have had a heart attack, probably not the first one, but this one was severe. Now you must let your family take care of you."

Eliza glanced around the darkened room. "Who is here?"

"Most of them are waiting outside in the hallway." Gilbert replied. "The rest are on their way. Soon you will have all of your children around you again."

By twelve noon, the next day, everyone had arrived at the hospital. Eliza seemed to be gaining strength, although her blood pressure began dropping slowly. Jules brought the Last Sacrament, and in the presence of his brothers and sisters he rubbed the sacred oil on his mother's forehead and eyes, then her lips and ears, and reaching underneath the sheets he dabbed her wrists. His lips barely moved as he recited the prayers for the sick and dying. All the while his eyes never left his mother's face.

Eliza could hear her children crying softly in the darkness. "Don't cry for me," she said, "I've had a good life, and a long one too. If God needs me soon then I will have to go, but until then we have this time to pray together and thank Him for all the blessings He has given to us."

Eliza fell into a deep sleep and when her breathing became more labored Millie asked Dr. Gilbert, "Is she suffering?"

"Look at her face," he replied. "She is smiling. A woman who looks like that cannot be suffering."

"Listen to the wind outside," Lloyd said. "It must be a storm."

Gabriel pulled the curtains aside. Shards of lightning lit up the sky and the rain fell sporadically against the window. "She always hated bad weather," he said. "It is good that she is asleep."

Jules watched Millie carefully and then pulled her aside and said, "Come with me. I have something to tell you."

They walked to the little chapel at the end of the hall. The pews were empty, and once the door shut behind them Jules and Millie could not hear any sound at all. Millie looked at the lighted candles in stands on either side of the statue of Jesus. He was holding His cloak aside, revealing His heart crowned with thorns and pierced by a sword. Millie ran her hand across His bare feet and looked into His glass eyes. She knew how His heart felt. Jules put his hand on her shoulder and motioned for her to sit down.

"I never wanted this time to come," he said. "It can't have been that long ago when we were little children and Mama was calling us to supper. She and I have been through many things together and she talked to me often. What I am about to tell you is something I learned from Mama several years ago. She told it to me in the strictest confidence and she also instructed me to tell the others when I thought the time was right."

"Why are you going to tell me without the others?" Millie asked.

"Because the time is not right for everyone to know," Jules replied. "But after tonight I may be the only one left who knows the secret, except Regina."

Millie's eyes grew wide. "Regina?"

Jules took a deep breath as he looked at his sister. "Regina is not Mama's child," he said, "but she is Papa's."

Millie did not say a word. She felt strange, as though this was the answer to questions that were always in the back of her mind. The way Regina looked. Her power over Oscar. The twinkle in Oscar's eyes whenever he saw her. The way she took care of him when he was dying.

"How can this be?" Millie whispered.

"Before Papa married Mama, he was married to Regina's mother. She died giving birth to Regina. After that, Grandma Daigle took care of her for a little while. Regina was still a baby when Mama and Papa got married. She thought Mama was her mother until she went to boarding school. A fellow student told her. That student was the niece of Regina's mother and had the same family name, Boudreau. Regina swore Papa and Mama to secrecy until it was appropriate to tell the other children that she was only a half sister. When Papa died Mama told me, and asked me to tell the others when the time was right."

Millie sat back in the pew. She could feel the cold, hard wood against her back. "For some reason, I am not surprised. It is as though there was something all along which held Mama, Papa and Regina together. I used to think it was because she was the first child, but it was more than that."

Jules picked up his sister's hand. "It doesn't matter anymore," he said. "She is just like us, always was and always will be. Mama made certain of that. Now that you know, you can decide what to do if something happens to me."

Millie looked at her brother. "There is another thing we need to discuss, the plantation."

"Yes," Jules said, "I know Mama wanted to divide the land before she died, but God has other things in mind for her. There will be time later for that."

~ ~ ~ ~

At midnight the nurse told the children it was not likely Eliza would awaken again. "Now is the time to tell her good-bye," she said. "She will hear you even though she seems to be asleep."

As her brothers and sisters whispered to Eliza, Millie watched, her eyes moving from face to face in that dark, warm hospital room. She imagined what it must have been like to be born, to be placed squealing into Eliza's waiting arms, and how soft her mother's breasts must have felt against her naked body. It was her turn now. Millie stood up and holding her handkerchief tightly she walked to the bed. "You can go now, Mama," Millie whispered. "Papa's built a new house for you and he's waiting."

Eliza suddenly opened her eyes and sat up in bed. "I go to Papa now," she said and fell back against her pillow.

~ ~ ~ ~

"Hurry Millie," Lloyd called out. "We need to get to the house before the others so we can open the door. All the food is set up and everyone will be hungry."

"Wait," Millie called back. "I have the key. I'm not ready to leave Mama yet!"

"Mama's already in heaven," Lloyd called back. "Come on!"

Lloyd left the cemetery and was walking, almost running now down the sidewalk past the Cathedral and the giant oak, past Tante Julie's house, and around the corner, where he stopped in front of Eliza's house and waited for his sister. Millie looked back at the sidewalk leading to the statue of the crucified Christ. She knew what Lloyd said was true. Eliza was not in that casket and soon everyone would be asked to leave and the burial would be finished. Millie shut her eyes tightly and decided she wanted to remember the casket covered with that enormous bouquet of flowers, hovering there above the open hole. She turned to the right and taking a short cut around the back of the church, she met up with Lloyd in the front yard. Millie handed the house key to him. He started to open the door and then stopped, and walking over to the bay window he peered through the glass.

"What are you looking at?" Millie asked.

Lloyd pointed to the window. She walked slowly toward him. It was high noon and sunlight spilled through the bay windows, across the floor of the parlor, engulfing Eliza's rocker in bright, white light.

ABOUT THE AUTHOR

Constance Monies is a freelance journalist and teacher, and a direct descendant of two of the original Acadian families to settle in Louisiana. Her love for the culture of her Cajun ancestors is reflected in her feature articles and stories that have appeared in newspapers and magazines across the Deep South. Constance and her husband Phil live in Lafayette, Louisiana – The Heart of Cajun Country.

Communicate with Constance and watch her videos at her blog: www.AHouseForEliza.com

CPSIA information can be obtained
at www.ICGtesting.com
Printed in the USA
LVHW052201060319
609799LV00001B/172